THE MISTRESS

FOXGLOVES REGENCY ROMANCE BOOK 1

K.P. MARCH

Book Cover by Luisa Galstyan

First Edition: April 2025

Identifiers: 979-8-9922989-0-1 (paperback); 979-8-9922989-1-8 (ebook)

❀ Created with Vellum

For the readers who like their fictional men a little damaged, a little gray, and with a bite

WARNING

The MMC of this story is dominant, flawed, and emotionally hurtful. If you're looking for a morally good hero, this isn't the man for you. He's damaged, afraid of love, and exhibits questionable behavior when confronted with it.

The FMC is his sweet, sensible, gentle counterpart. She is not to be considered weak, though, because of her nature. In many ways, she is the core of strength in this story.

This is a standalone book in an interconnected series. Guaranteed HEA. You will see Amelia and Gideon again as side characters in future books.

AMELIA

1808, COVENTRY, ENGLAND

Clutching the fresh bouquet of foxgloves in her hand, Amelia knocked gently on the aged wooden door with her other. Upon hearing the soft permission to enter, she pushed it open and spotted her sister upright in bed, pulling her sniffling pink nose out of her latest novel.

"I'm off," Amelia told her. "Is there anything you need from the Estate?"

Lydia, five years Amelia's junior, answered, "Another novel. I'm just about finished with this one, and Thomas should be able to pick one I haven't read yet." She turned back to the near finished tome in her hand. "And do tell Thomas to stop his worrying. I'm perfectly fine. He's been fussing so much, one would think I was on my deathbed."

Amelia fought her smile. "He worries because he cares," she offered.

Lydia turned her beautiful face, so like her sister's, back to her. They both shared the same heart shaped faces, but Lydia was softer, lighter, her face slightly rounder. And with her golden hair, blue eyes, and high, sweet voice, she possessed an angelic quality to her features that Amelia did not.

"He cares about you, too, but he doesn't lose his mind when you get sick," she countered irritably.

Amelia almost let her laugh out. Lydia was correct, of course. Yes, Thomas cared about Amelia. And yes, he worried more for Lydia. But it wasn't Amelia's place to state the obvious. Not today, at least.

Thomas Colbrook, the Earl of Coventry, was more their family than anything else. His father had been close friends with Amelia and Lydia's father, John Becham. When the late earl died suddenly in a hunting accident mere weeks after Thomas was born, John vowed the new little earl would never feel the loss of a father so long as he lived. A sentiment made all the stronger as the years passed and he sired no son of his own.

Shortly after Thomas's birth, Amelia was born. The two grew up side by side and could not have been more brother and sister had they, in fact, shared the same blood. The Dowager Countess of Coventry was a kind woman, and she loved and welcomed Amelia like her own daughter. Five years later, when Amelia's mother died bringing Lydia into the world, Adelaide Colbrook showered even more love on the girls, filling in the space of mother, and raised them to be proper ladies. She died, however, when Amelia was only fifteen and before she could launch either girl into Society as she had wanted. John, for his part, didn't participate in the workings of the *ton*. He taught all three children the value of hard work and independence. And both parents instilled in them the value of family, in all its shapes and sizes, and loving each other deeply.

Lydia's birth didn't just inspire tenderness from the adults, though. Thomas and Amelia, six and five at the time, respectively, felt a profound protectiveness for the tiniest thing they'd ever seen in their short lives. One who had come into the world with such sadness. They smothered her from the start, and while the girls became proper sisters as Lydia grew, Thomas and Lydia never quite became siblings. Their relationship turned into another kind of love. One they had yet to acknowledge or declare, but one everyone else could see plain as day.

Adults now twenty years later, all parents having passed away, the trio remained close as ever. Thomas visited the cottage multiple times a week, and the ladies visited the Coventry Estate just as regularly. They would come and go from each home as easily as if they belonged to both, which, of course, they did. But one tradition that had established itself at the care of John and Adelaide was a weekly formal dinner. Their parents began this tradition when Lydia was still barely a babe as a way to instill the importance of regularly pausing with their family.

It was to this dinner Amelia was departing, leaving a sick Lydia at home. She decided to ignore Lydia's comment on how differently Thomas fussed over each sister and replied instead, "I'll be sure to bring you a book."

Lydia rolled her eyes but thanked her, and Amelia's smile broke through as she closed the bedroom door, shaking her head.

Amelia made her way downstairs and out the front door of their old, perfectly maintained cottage. Both the homey interior and stone exterior were cozy and welcoming, and the garden that grew along the front of their home added life and vibrancy to the whole structure. Walking past it, she climbed on to the front of the ridiculous carriage Thomas insisted they use when he assumed responsibility for their household after John's passing. Both women had protested it was completely unnecessary with the Estate being less than a ten minute walk from the cottage, but he had not been swayed.

She sat down next to Walters, their butler and all-around house man, rather than riding in the carriage by herself. He and

Mrs. Nichols, their housekeeper and cook, were the full of their little household and had been with the Bechams since they were little girls. They didn't need more than them as all three kids rolled up their own sleeves whenever needed.

"How is Miss Lydia doing?" Walters asked in his old gruff voice, moving the carriage forward.

"Better," Amelia answered. "I'm sure she'll be back to normal in the next few days. She's complaining, though, about Thomas's excessive concern." Amelia looked over to see Walters chuckling, matching her own amusement.

"Those two," he agreed. "When they'll finally get their heads out of the sand, we have yet to see. Going on ten years waiting for them."

"Ten years?" Amelia repeated, a bit shocked. "Lydia was ten, Walters."

"Believe me, we all saw it then. Maybe it was too soon, yes, and they didn't know, but we did. She just had a bit of growing up to do. So did the little earl. We thought when she was fifteen, they'd figure it out, but still nothing, and now she's twenty," he shook his head in disappointment.

"I intend to force their hand this year. It's been long enough. I'll give them a few more months before I finally let the secret out," Amelia shared her plan.

"You'll do no such thing," Walters scolded. "Mind your own affairs, Miss Amelia. Let them build their own story."

"Hmm," Amelia replied noncommittally. Walters understood, of course, and pursed his lips at her stubbornness.

They arrived at the large and regal Coventry Estate, and Amelia bid Walters goodbye. She made her way up the stone front steps, letting herself in. Hughes, the Coventry Estate butler, never observed protocol with the Bechams as they had practically grown up at the Estate. She knew Thomas would be waiting in the drawing room for the Becham ladies to arrive, so she made her way there without delay. Crossing through the luxurious entry hall, her steps light atop the extravagant rug, all was as it should be until she opened the door to the drawing room.

Light from the setting sun still peeked through the large windows across from the door, making the creams, pale colors, and light golds of the tastefully decorated room seem brighter. She found Thomas standing up from the pale, intricately embroidered couch facing the fireplace.

But he wasn't the only one.

In the matching armchair beside him, facing her head on, was the most beautiful man Amelia had ever seen gracefully rising to his feet. He was tall, well-built, and broad shouldered under his clearly expensive clothing. His dark hair fell in short, loose waves around a tanned face. She was immediately riveted to that face, admiring the sharp cut of exquisite cheekbones, a straight nose, and chiseled jawline. His harsh masculinity stole her breath away and made her palms start to sweat where she still held the gold doorknob. His thin lips were surrounded by the light hints of a beard, like he hadn't shaved in a day or two. Amelia couldn't explain why her mouth watered at the sight.

His severe beauty registered, but then she met his almond shaped eyes. Bright green emeralds captivated and tore through her, cataloguing each reaction she had and more. Her heart began beating wildly in answer, as if it wanted to reach him. She found herself unable to pull her gaze away from those eyes that saw straight through to her soul before even bothering to pause at her face.

"Ah, Amelia," she was barely aware of Thomas speaking. "Come meet Gideon Edwards."

Gideon.

"The Duke of Birmingham."

That caught Amelia's attention. Her eyes snapped to Thomas. His perpetually cheerful face, with blonde hair, pale blue eyes, and a forever smile, suggested he hadn't noticed Amelia's raging reaction to his companion.

She looked back at the starkly handsome man, whose face remained politely impassive but eyes gleamed at her knowingly. And she swore she felt those eyes like a tether wrap around her, pulling her, binding her directly to him. *A duke.*

GIDEON

*G*ideon watched the young woman still standing in the doorway continue to struggle. She had yet to say a word or move since laying eyes on him, and he, too, couldn't find it in himself to look away. She was striking, with light brown hair that looked like burnt gold spun into silk. Her large eyes were the softest brown he'd ever seen, surrounded by high cheekbones, a delicately pert nose, and a finely strong jawline. She was at once both soft and defined. And those full, pouted lips had his mind wandering to thoughts not fit for polite company. Her face boasted a lovely flush that ran down her neck, and his blood stirred as he regarded her slim, yet still deliciously curvy figure – even wrapped in the slightly outdated, clearly worn dress as it currently was. In a word, she was breathtaking.

And the way those eyes clung to his did things to him. Like he was both her storm and her life raft.

"Gideon," his friend, Thomas, continued, either oblivious or uncaring of what was transpiring between him and this brazen creature who had just strolled right in. "Miss Amelia Becham."

Ah. Well, her entry made more sense then. This was the Earl

of Coventry's infamous mistress. Everyone knew about the all but reclusive earl and the family he supported. Indeed, Thomas's disinterest in the workings of Society and lack of convention were why he and Gideon were friends to begin with. It wasn't uncommon to have a mistress, of course, but to shun Society for her and her family's company alone was less common. The woman, Amelia, had never been seen – Thomas was quite secretive about it, not even mentioning her to Gideon – but it was well known she had been close with the Colbrook family for many years before taking up her current position two years ago after her father's passing. Gideon didn't blame or judge her. In fact, he respected any person willing to do what needed to be done to survive and care for their family. Clearly, she made a smart arrangement as Thomas not only supported her, but also her supposedly sweet and innocent younger sister and their entire household.

Looking at her now, still frozen in the doorway, he began to understand why. Gideon would easily spend that and more on such a captivating woman.

"Amelia?" Thomas spoke. "Are you alright?"

Gideon watched the young woman forcibly pull her eyes from him and turn towards her benefactor. He'd be lying if he said he wasn't pleased to see her reacting so strongly to him, especially in front of Thomas. Within moments of meeting him, something in her was instinctively responding to him – just as he was identifying a similar feeling in himself. Almost like she was his.

He shook the thought away quickly.

Gideon watched her visibly gather herself and stand up straighter, and he couldn't fight the smile that tugged at his lips when he considered the futility of it. Her light chocolate eyes turned back to him with determination as she finally strode forward, a cluster of flowers swinging from one hand.

"Your Grace," she said once she stood before him, dipping

into a flawless curtsy. Her voice wasn't high as he'd been expecting, but low and just the right edge of husky. Gideon felt his cock twitch in answer.

He took her free hand and bent to place a kiss to the back of it, his skin tingling where it met hers. She shivered at his touch.

"Miss Becham," Gideon's voice came out rough. "What lovely flowers."

She took her hand back and looked down at the other as if only now remembering she held a bouquet of foxgloves there. She stepped to Thomas's side with a quiet "thank you," the blush on her face brightening all the way down to her neckline.

Gideon wanted to trace that blush with his fingers.

What was wrong with him? This was his friend's longstanding mistress. She wasn't open to being pursued.

And yet, he couldn't stop his mind, body, and something deeper from responding to her. There was something about this woman – available or not, Thomas's mistress or not – that was calling to him in a way no other had.

"I'm sorry to intrude, Thomas." Bold. Not only walking into his home as if it were her own, but calling her titled benefactor by his Christian name in front of another peer of the realm.

His amusement grew.

"I didn't realize you were previously engaged," she continued. Her voice was confident, but Gideon noticed how she pointedly avoided looking at him. He could feel her awareness of him, though, fight it as she might.

"Nonsense," Thomas said cheerfully. "Gideon stopped by to see the mare I recently acquired, and I invited him to join us for dinner."

Gideon hadn't known Thomas's mistress would be joining, but he was glad she was and that he'd decided to stay.

She glanced at him, the nervousness beneath her confidence easier to spot in her eyes. "I'm sure I couldn't disturb you both further," she replied. "I shall leave you to dine without me."

"Why?" Thomas's face pulled in confusion. "You're not disturbing us. If anything, Gideon is the disruption," he smiled good-naturedly at his friend. Gideon rolled his eyes at him. "You'll stay," he said back to his mistress. *Amelia.*

She pursed her lips, glancing again in Gideon's direction, clearly not pleased with the command. Thomas hadn't yet noticed her reaction to his other guest, and Gideon was sure the young woman wanted to keep it that way. Likely the reason for her attempt at a quick exit.

Time for Gideon to join in. He didn't want her to leave.

"I'd be honored if you would stay, Miss Becham," Gideon said seductively, "and allow me to intrude on your previously laid plan."

She met his eyes and swallowed. Her eyes were less helpless now, settling into her response to him, and she looked at him with understanding and some scrutiny, testing the edges of the challenge he presented her. She could tell it was a test, and she was cautiously interested.

My God, he absolutely understood why Thomas barely participated in Society, opting to spend his days with her, taking on the burden of her family for years. Not only was she beautiful beyond measure, she was at once the perfect balance of alluring, yet vulnerable; seductive, yet submissive; experienced, yet innocent. Who in the world was she, and what did he need to do to obtain her?

The back of his mind still protested, not wanting to cause insult to his only real friend in the *ton*, but that voice was getting quieter the longer he watched this woman.

"Very well, Your Grace," she said, her eyes still on him, and he gave her an approving grin.

She didn't offer one back.

"Now that's settled," Thomas said, rubbing his hands together before extending an arm to his mistress. "Shall we?" Taking it, Amelia turned away from Gideon and proceeded to the dining room. Gideon felt his eyes narrow and mouth thin at the contact. He didn't like their easy familiarity, and he didn't like Thomas touching this woman.

He fell into step behind them, following their lead to the large dining room, which was lit by the warm glow of several candles. She paused in the doorway to hand the flowers in her hand to Thomas's butler, who stood just inside the room.

"They're from the cottage, Hughes," she told him, obviously preoccupied.

"Very good, Miss Becham," he took the offered bouquet, unfazed. As if this was a normal occurrence during the mistress's visits. She must be quite comfortable here, indeed.

Gideon stepped forward and pulled out a chair for her, taking her by surprise.

She took her seat at the elegantly set table with another murmured word of thanks. He saw her blush, which had since calmed, return fiercely at his proximity. Gideon inhaled her warm, soft vanilla scent, and his blood heated in response even as it soothed him.

Thomas took his place at the head of the table, while Gideon strode around it to sit across from her on Thomas's other side. He had yet to spare his friend more than a few glances since the beauty walked in. His eyes stayed trained on her, and while she struggled to keep hers away, he knew she could feel it. Feel him.

Whatever this was between them, it was clearly potent and well beyond attraction. He planned to explore the full depth and pull of it as much as he could while in her presence.

AMELIA

ood Lord, what was happening to her? Who was this man, and why was she feeling so deeply connected to him having only just met? What in heavens was going on?

She could feel his eyes blazing a trail of heat along her skin. Her spine tingled in response, and her heart had yet to find its normal rhythm since she'd laid eyes on the Duke of Birmingham. And when he'd touched her, his hand felt unexpectedly rough for a Duke, while his lips were soft but firm in their pressure. God, she was still overheated from the awareness that had shot through her at the contact.

"How is Lydia?" Thomas asked, pulling her from her reverie, the concern in his tone evident.

Amelia cleared her throat and tried to find her way back to common sense and propriety.

"Much better," she turned in her seat and forced her focus to center on Thomas seated beside her, ignoring the tingles running down the back of her neck. "She'll be right as rain in the next day or so, I expect."

"Thank goodness," Thomas's heavy sigh would have made

Amelia roll her eyes if she wasn't so on edge. Heavens, he did act like Lydia was dangerously ill, not down with a common cold.

"She did bid you stop your worrying," Amelia prodded, as they all filled their plates with the food the footmen served. She began to feel on slightly more solid ground speaking easily with Thomas and going through their regular motions.

It wasn't to last, though. The powerful male wrapped in riches across from her forced all her attention back to him. What little she had managed to redirect that is.

"Who is Lydia?" his deep velvet voice caressed her skin. She tried to fight the shiver that ran in its wake and failed. Once again turning to his fiercely masculine face, with features artists could easily spend their entire lives trying to capture, she latched back onto those bright, probing green eyes that held her in an iron grip.

"My sister, Your Grace," her voice felt breathy addressing him when only a moment ago it had been sure. She hoped the duke didn't noticed. Who was she kidding? Of course, he did. Something about this man seemed inherently attuned to her and all that she was. She simplified her hope, instead, to Thomas not noticing whatever this deeply intimate connection was between his two guests.

"Ah," he replied. "And she is ill?"

"Just a cold, Your Grace." Why was she so jittery speaking to him? She couldn't understand the nerves coursing through her, but she had the sense that he, at least, did. "Nothing serious."

She forced herself to act like everything was normal and eat, taking small bites, but she was unable to taste the deliciously aromatic food.

"Well, I hope she recovers soon as you expect," he said both kindly and politely. And yet the current between them, his force of will, her yielding, were anything but proper.

"Thank you, Your Grace," her voice was soft. Putting down

her fork and knife, she picked up her glass and took a fortifying drink of wine.

There was a blissful pause for a few moments, during which the only noise was the sound of cutlery against the fine china. Amelia kept her eyes steadfastly fixed on either her plate or the lovely centerpiece of bright flowers that popped against the white tablecloth between her and the duke. She chewed her food with forced calm.

"How old is she?" The Duke of Birmingham broke the silence, continuing the conversation as if there had been no lull.

Amelia looked up. "Lydia? She is twenty."

"And how old are you?" Again, he spoke with perfect politeness, but the tug she felt towards him changed even the most mundane of conversations into an intimacy she had never experienced before.

"I am twenty-five, Your Grace." Her hands had stopped moving as she answered his questions. Why was she feeling so warm?

"And it is just you two?" he asked, not stopping in his own eating as he continued to probe.

"Yes, Your Grace," she answered. "And Thomas."

"Hmm," he pursed his lips.

She could feel his displeasure as sure as her own confusion at it. She didn't know what caused it, or why she even cared, but she felt an immediate need to fix it. Some part of her wanted to please him. This new part he had clearly unearthed and drawn forth just by existing and meeting her. A part that felt as much her as any other.

It didn't make sense. Nor did she know how to fix whatever had caused his unhappiness. So, she stayed silent and tried to turn back to her food.

She chanced a glance at Thomas, and to her dismay, he was watching them curiously, brow furrowed. Apparently, his previous obliviousness had not held fast.

She would have to deal with his questions later, she knew, but for now, she had to get a damn grip on herself and make it through this meal. Everything else, Thomas, his curiosity, the warmth that had yet to subside, the desire to please this stranger so profoundly above her station, the cord she felt between them…. That could all wait to be dealt with later.

"Your parents?" that rough velvet voice spoke.

"Your Grace?" She looked back at him to find his cutlery abandoned as he held his glass of wine halfway to his mouth.

"What of your parents?" he clarified before taking a drink. She watched his throat work on the swallow, and she had to compose herself before answering.

"They are no longer with us," she shared. "Our mother died giving birth to Lydia, and our father joined her two years ago."

The grief of losing her father had calmed, but she still felt it every day. His loss and the loss of Thomas's mother still weighed on Amelia, as she was sure they did on Lydia and Thomas, as well.

"We were lucky to have been granted so much time with them," Amelia heard herself sharing without prompting. She swallowed, reaching for her wine and shaking her head lightly at the inappropriateness of her offering.

"Them?" The duke's voice held a tenderness to it, and she met the emerald traps that were his eyes. The softness she observed there told her he saw the sadness she carried with as much clarity as he seemed to see the rest of her.

Who was this man, she wondered yet again, and how did she know with such certainty how well he saw her? She knew she would keep asking herself these questions for the rest of her days until she finally had the answers. She was never going to forget the Duke of Birmingham.

"Yes, Your Grace," she answered him still in a soft, intimate voice. Both of their food and wine now sat forgotten, and Thomas's unusual silence made it all the easier to forget he, too, was there. "Our father and the Dowager Countess of Coventry. She left us some years before our father. When I was fifteen."

"You were close with the dowager countess?" he inquired.

"Yes, Your Grace," Amelia replied. "She was, for all intents and purposes, our mother. She raised us."

"I see," he said, his face inscrutable, and she couldn't even begin to fathom what he was thinking.

Abruptly, the enthralling duke stood and stepped towards Thomas, clapping a hand on his shoulder. "Well, I must be going," he spoke, his eyes still fixed on Amelia. "Thank you for showing me your mare, Thomas. She is truly beyond compare." The way those eyes watched her made Amelia think he wasn't talking about the horse. "And for the meal. It is the best I've had in memory."

"You're sure you must leave so soon?" Thomas asked his friend, speaking for the first time in what felt like an age.

Oh, dear. Thomas was scheming.

"I'm afraid so," the duke replied. "But I'm sure I will see you soon." He rounded the table to where Amelia was still seated, gently taking her hand, causing that current to once again course through her from the point where his skin met hers. Her heart stuttered and then ricocheted into a gallop.

He pressed those soft lips to her hand as he had earlier, and Amelia's tongue shot out on reflex to lick her lips at the feel of the gentle pressure. She was struck with the sudden desire to feel those lips on hers, and that thought was so new to her, she lost all sense of how to respond.

"It was a pleasure, Miss Becham." His touch, the seductive voice, the penetrating green eyes, and his warm, spiced scent overwhelmed her senses. Her hand gripped his tighter, whether to keep hold of herself or him, she wasn't sure. She was overcome with an impending sense of loss for this man so far above her, yet somehow, she was sure he was something to her. Something vital and important. This she knew as well as she knew herself. And she wasn't sure she'd ever see him again.

As if he could read her thoughts, which she wildly thought he might, he whispered so softly only she could hear, "We will meet again soon, Amelia."

It was a promise, and it settled deep in her bones, calming the unusual panic she was beginning to feel at his departure.

Understanding lit his eyes as if he could feel the emotions rolling through her, and she registered his pleasure at how she responded to him. As if he was the composer, and she was his symphony.

She settled further, both in his promise and his pleasure.

GIDEON

*S*he was his. Gideon knew it. He had to have her. He could talk with Thomas and make him understand. Thomas was a good man – and if Amelia Becham agreed, he wouldn't stand in the way of their happiness.

Gideon knew he had to leave. Sitting there much longer would have exposed what was between him and the mistress in a most unfavorable manner. No, Thomas had to be treated with respect and friendship as Gideon took over the care of his mistress.

Even more than that, he realized. Riding back to his Estate, he thought over what the young woman had revealed – the Dowager Countess of Coventry had been a mother figure to the Becham women growing up. This was more than just convenient employment for Amelia Becham. It seemed she might have been groomed to be Thomas's mistress from childhood.

Hopefully, her fondness and loyalty for the earl wouldn't prevent her from severing the relationship and entering into an arrangement with Gideon. Even as he thought back to how she responded to him, his hands gripped the reins harder in jealousy. No, he reasoned with himself, thinking in particular of how she yielded to him so naturally and calmed at his murmured promise to see her again. No, whatever feelings she had for Thomas, this mistress felt something powerful with Gideon.

He would still take care to woo her properly, of course. She deserved as much, and it would quiet her mind, making it easier for her to follow through on what she already seemed to sense and leave Thomas. It would also ease the hit to Thomas's pride, should there be any, if she moved away from him slowly, showing their relationship had simply run its course. And once he had her unfettered agreement, Gideon would talk to Thomas.

Thomas had been Gideon's good friend for the past six years. Ever since he'd taken up the mantle of the Duke of Birmingham at twenty-six. Gideon had spent the better part of his young adulthood abroad, having run away at seventeen almost the very moment his mother had finally died. Watching her spend her life under the constant, crushing weight of her sadness, Gideon had tried – tried and tried and tried – to bring some joy to her life. He'd loved her beyond what had been healthy for a child, shouldering the burden of her happiness, and he showered her with his love in his childish innocence, thinking it would be enough. That it was all she needed. But it never was. The cold indifference with which his father treated her had always outweighed anything Gideon or Genevieve could ever do. Although, his sister never got the chance to feel the burden of their mother's happiness and the guilt of her sadness since she'd died with Genevieve was only one.

On its heels, though, Gideon also bore the weight of leaving his sister for nine years with the bastard that had sired them. But Gideon couldn't have helped it. He couldn't spend another moment under the same roof as the man that had given him his life, his future, and – in Gideon's eye – had all but killed their mother with his neglect. Genevieve had survived, and since his return, he had found in her a much more open recipient for his affections. She had suffered a home devoid of care, warmth, and parental love in her short life, and on the other side of the same coin, Gideon had spent his young life having his love constantly rejected and found wanting. In offering his brotherly affections to his sister, he was rewarded with her acceptance and love in return.

That was the only love Gideon believed in – the love a brother bore for a sister, and hers in return. The love that parents bore for children was foreign to him, and the love between husbands and wives – well, he didn't believe such a thing was even possible. And so, he grew into a man that knew he would never marry. He couldn't remember ever consciously making the decision. He simply grew up and felt the knowledge grow with him. If Genevieve never gave him a nephew to serve as his heir, however, he might be forced to consider marriage, but even in that case, he knew with certainty that he would never love his wife, nor would she love him. It was simply impossible. A fact that left him with sadness when he considered Genevieve's fate with her future husband. But that was just how marriages were. A quality in their nature. He would ensure she found a partner that took care of her and treated her with respect. And in the very unlikely event he also married, he would give the same to his own wife. Something their father failed to bestow on their mother.

He arrived at Birmingham Estate and upon entering, heard the music filling his home. He cut straight to the drawing room to greet his sister, covering the large, darkly colored entry hall in quick strides as he breathed in the warm spiced scent edged with florals.

Birmingham Estate was grander, older, and felt significantly darker than Coventry Estate. Where his friend's home had balanced hints of dark luxury with lightness and openness in its furnishings, his home was rich and dark, covered in decadent wealth at every corner. From the intricately patterned wallpapers or wooden walls, the detailed doors and bannisters, and the delicate gold trim lining every room throughout the house. It was beautiful. It had always been beautiful, even when it felt cold and loveless during his childhood. Now, though, with his parents long gone, the dark paneled wood around the entire estate; the deep greens, reds, browns of the walls and furnishings; the rich golds of their inherited wealth; the plush carpets and heady scent were welcoming and warm.

Stepping inside the drawing room, he spotted Genevieve seated at the old pianoforte, deep in her composition. He and his sister shared many of the same features and the same dark hair, but where his eyes were bright green, hers were dark and currently riveted to the piano keys.

She was vastly skilled in her music, and he was pleased to see the joy it brought her, losing herself in the beauty she created. She had surpassed the skill of her governess early on, and Gideon had promptly hired an instructor to help her further develop the talent.

He made his way to the large, maroon armchair facing her and sat down. The room enveloped him in its warm comfort, the red patterned wallpaper and glowing candles surrounding him like a blanket. He relaxed with one ankle crossed over his knee and watched her play, enjoying the notes of her creation as he waited for her to finish.

"How was the horse?" she asked, not missing a note as she spoke.

Perhaps she wasn't as lost to the piece as he'd assumed.

"Very fine," Gideon answered. "But I found myself preoccupied during my visit."

"Oh?" Genevieve brought the piece to a close and turned on the bench to face him more directly. "By what?"

"Nothing that concerns you," he said firmly.

"Then why bring it up?" she griped, her face pinching in irritation.

"You are right," he replied, because she was. "I shouldn't have mentioned it. But now that I have, suffice it say that I found more than just a beautiful mare at the Coventry Estate, and I had a very enjoyable meal."

"You are being purposely coy to bait me, brother," she scolded, turning back to her piano and clearly dismissing him. "And I find I do not like it at all, nor does it suit you."

Gideon chuckled. His sixteen-year-old sister had more sense and composure than most adults thrice her age, and she hadn't even launched into Society yet.

"Perhaps you are right," he said over the music coming once again from her skilled hands. "I do apologize."

She scoffed in reply and continued playing. "Call for some tea, then," she said.

Gideon smiled as she accepted his apologize. He stood and made his way to the fireplace, pulling the cord to call for tea. He resumed his seat and let his thoughts wander under the melody filling the room.

Today had turned into a much better day than he anticipated when he first woke up that morning. He thought back to those beautiful, unusually light brown eyes, looking at him like he was her destruction and her salvation.

Their tea was brought in, and Gideon thanked their maid as Genevieve kept playing. He poured two cups and relaxed back with his, letting the notes fill his soul.

No, he would never marry, but he would find happiness and fulfillment. With someone who recognized him for who and what he was, and that fit him with who and what she was. And with the blazing connection he had felt between him and Amelia, their visceral attraction, the push and pull, he felt sure he had found her.

Gideon strengthened his plan as he sipped his tea. Genevieve finished the piece and joined him on the couch beside his armchair, accepting the cup he handed her from the small table. He felt easy in his resolve.

All would proceed as it should, as he wanted. He reveled in the thoughts of having her, and having her soon. He would care for her for the rest of his life, he had no doubt. The power of their connection was so fierce, so potent – she had to have been made for him, and he for her. He could feel it in the marrow of his bones.

AMELIA

"Amelia," Thomas broke the heavy silence following the Duke of Birmingham's exit.

"I don't know," Amelia stared at the door the duke had just exited through, still reeling.

"What don't you know?"

"I don't know what just happened," she shook her head trying in vain to clear her thoughts as she faced him. She was annoyed to find an obnoxious grin on his face.

"You're interested in him," Thomas explained.

"It's impossible," she tried to remind them both.

"Why?" he pushed. They still sat at the table, but neither one of them made a move to eat, drink, or leave, having their discussion right there. "You like him, and from what I could see, the feeling was very much mutual. You've never shown an interest in anyone before, Amelia, and truth be told, you two are actually quite well-suited for one another. He's a bit willful and sometimes seems cold, but he's a great man, intelligent, and exceedingly kind. He cares deeply. More than any man I've ever met before. He has much in common with you."

"Thomas," she paused for emphasis. "He's a duke."

"So, what?" he argued. "He doesn't hold store by Society's rules, which is how he and I became such good friends. And I have gathered that he is not overly fond of his title."

Amelia's curiosity piqued. "Why not?"

"His father was not a kind man from what I've heard, though not directly from him," Thomas said somberly. "Gideon had a troubled relationship with both him and his mother. It's said his mother was a sad, withdrawn woman because of her husband's cruelty, and she was unable to show Gideon much affection as a result. He and his sister were left to their father's harsh care and teachings, and he grew up hating the burden of the title and its association with the man."

"Goodness," Amelia breathed, her heart hurting at the thought of the strong, confident man she met being raised in such pain. "How do you know this?"

"The gossips talk," Thomas shrugged.

"The poor man. Even so, he is still the Duke of Birmingham. Nothing can come of our interest."

"The hell it can't," she noted the steel of stubbornness glinting in her friend's eye. "I think he is perfect for you, and title or not, you are a good match for him. You both are strong, generous, and have good heads on your shoulders. In fact, I'm quite shocked it hadn't occurred to me before now. And if anyone can bring love into his stark world, it would be you. You will make him a fine duchess and even finer wife."

"Thomas…," she began, shock ringing in her voice. Her? A duchess? He had lost his damned mind.

"Amelia," he shook his head with finality, cutting her off. "I have never pushed you to find a husband or come out. But this I will push because you want it, too, and he will make you happy. What's more, I think you can make him happy and, together, can heal what his parents broke in him."

"You have lost your mind," she voiced her earlier thought. "I knew a day would come when we'd see it go, but I hadn't expected quite so spectacular a departure."

"Joke all you want, sister," he rolled his eyes at her, not to be deterred. "But you will be marrying the Duke of Birmingham. I promise you."

Outwardly, Amelia sighed to let Thomas know how foolish she thought him. Inwardly, however, his words nestled into her heart and mind, planting an uncharacteristic seed of want and hope for the future he seemed to be picturing so clearly.

She had always imagined she would wed. In some far off future, she eventually expected to have a husband and children. Lydia and Thomas would marry and perhaps find her a suitable partner once they were settled. But she'd never before met a man and *wanted* to join lives with him, nor had she expected to. That was, until today. It felt like an impossible dream, but Thomas's conviction and the duke's singular attentions had her starting to believe. And then there were these new parts of herself she could feel awakening. Parts that felt so much like the truth of who and what she was and that had only been waiting for him. Perhaps it was all meant to be. Perhaps she was meant to marry Gideon Edwards.

Still, the more logical part of her countered, "I have nothing to offer him, though. No money, no title, no connections."

"Stop that," Thomas said in a stern tone. "You have money. I'll settle a generous dowry on you, and that will be *yours*. He has his own money, title, and connections. What more could he need of that? What he *needs* is love and a partner. A true one. Who could better give him that than you?"

"He doesn't even know me, though," that insidiously reasonable voice spoke again.

"He will. Once Lydia is better, we'll need to get you both some dresses," Thomas began plotting.

"What? What for?" she asked with both dread and a sliver of excitement that she was logically trying to deny.

"You'll need some dresses and evening gowns for London. We'll join the Season and that will give you and Gideon ample opportunities to interact. He can then begin his official courtship."

"London? Do you actually think he'd follow us there?" she asked, a bit skeptical.

"I'll make sure of it. I'll tell him of our plans and that I intend to introduce you and Lydia to Society. I have not the slightest doubt he'd follow us."

She reached a hand forward and began spinning the stem of her wineglass on the table as she considered what Thomas was suggesting. To think, just this morning, it had been a normal day, and now they were trying to orchestrate her marriage. To a duke, no less.

She asked somewhat nervously, "Are you really quite certain we should be doing this? It's been some years since Lydia and I have been to Town, and we have never been to any of the Season's events or balls at all. You know this."

"I do," he nodded, "and I've only attended the very few that were unavoidable. But I learned enough from them to know Mother prepared you both well. It will chafe, but she did indeed give us the lessons we need to navigate the *ton*."

"Very well."

She still couldn't help the anxiety building inside her at the prospect of attending Society's events, and she took up her glass again for a slightly more generous sip.

But she trusted Thomas, she thought to herself. This may also present the opportunity at last for Lydia and Thomas to grow their relationship. As the Season progressed, she would encourage their interactions and, with gentle but persistent pressure, force them both to begin acknowledging their own feelings.

Her plotting on Thomas and Lydia's behalf helped settle her nerves. As much as she wanted to see the duke again, the plans centering around herself felt rather daunting. Let Thomas focus on setting up her future. She would focus on setting up his and Lydia's.

"And once he's spent a bit of public time with you," Thomas continued, finally picking up his own glass and leaning back in his chair, completely oblivious to Amelia's thoughts, "he'll seek my permission to court you. From there, it should be quick to arrive at an engagement. Before the end of the Season, to be sure, if not much sooner."

"You're getting ahead of yourself," Amelia commented, knowing full well she was, as well. She was imagining a similar timeline for Thomas and her sister.

"Trust me. Gideon is not one to delay when there's something he wants," Thomas chuckled. "He is both stubborn and relentless. I wouldn't be surprised if you're fully married in the next three months."

"Thomas, for Heaven's sake," Amelia rolled her eyes. "Let's just take this a step at a time, shall we? Stop planning my wedding. Dresses and attending the right parties, alright? Let's focus on that for now."

"You focus on it," he advised. "I'll do as I please."

GIDEON

*S*itting back and savoring his brandy in the dark, smoky room of the gentleman's club, Gideon was still drunk from meeting the lovely Amelia Becham two days prior. Even Genevieve had been sensing a difference in him these days since – his constant smiles, elated mood – though she hadn't said a word. Living with their father had taught her a super-human power of observation and ability to assess her surround-ings. Gideon knew she noted his evident happiness and excitement, and was monitoring it keenly.

As he sat, lost to his own pleasant thoughts of his plans, Thomas walked in and, spotting Gideon, beelined to join him.

"Well met," Thomas said, taking a seat beside him.

"Thomas," Gideon replied.

There was a pause, during which Thomas was promptly served a drink and Gideon's was refreshed, and then Thomas asked, "How are you, my friend?"

There was a mischief in his eye, but admittedly, it was hard to really tell since Thomas always seemed to have a mischievous glint to him. If Gideon had ever had a brother, he would have both enjoyed and likely hated having one like Thomas.

"I am quite well," Gideon took another sip. "And you? How has your other dinner guest been?"

Thomas's face split into a grin at Gideon's question. "Oh, we are both 'quite well,' too, I'd say. Although, Amelia might be a touch better. Much like you, I imagine."

Thomas was baiting him, and Gideon felt a wariness take hold within him. Was Thomas trying to encourage Gideon? Or was he calling out Gideon's inappropriate behavior towards his mistress at his own dinner table? He'd never known Thomas to be an indirect man, but then again, Gideon had never disrespected him, nor tried to take anything of his before, let alone something as unmistakably precious as Amelia. But it seemed too far-fetched to think Thomas *wanted* to be rid of her.

Gideon decided on a cautious approach. "I am glad to hear it," was all he said, not taking the bait.

"I won't beat around the bush, Birmingham," like Gideon thought, Thomas was a direct man. "I will be taking Amelia and Lydia to London in a few days' time to join the Season. We plan to attend the Welsey's Ball at the end of this week, as well as accept all other invitations we receive."

Gideon's mind went into overdrive as he stared at the reclining earl and read between the lines of what he was saying. Thomas wasn't telling him this information by way of idle conversation. He was informing him of their plan so Gideon could adjust his accordingly. But what Gideon was still unsure of was *why*.

He stared unseeingly across the room, taking a mindless drink of his brandy. He could easily figure their participation this Season was to launch the younger girl, Lydia, into Society, assuming Amelia had asked him to find her sister a husband. It was unconventional, dare Gideon say *improper*, to bring one's mistress into Society and try to marry off her sister, but it wasn't impossible. And Thomas was a far cry from conventional.

But did Thomas want *Gideon* to marry the girl? He wondered as he swirled the liquid in his glass. Thomas couldn't possibly expect that. Perhaps he wanted Gideon to employ her as Thomas did Amelia, and this was an excuse to get them to meet and spend time together.

But then why had Thomas been baiting him about Amelia?

Was he really trying to rid himself of Amelia and saw an opportunity in Gideon and Amelia's reactions to each other the other day? Perhaps he wanted to pursue the younger girl himself, considering the way he'd asked after her at dinner. That would be extremely convenient. More than that, he admitted to himself, it would be ideal. Gideon would happily, *happily*, take over the care of Amelia Becham. In fact, he fully intended to, whether Thomas was on board with it or not, but he had been planning on a more nuanced approach. But if his musings proved correct, it would be far more direct and expedient.

He would need more time to be sure of Thomas's intent, though, and that time would be in London. And if Thomas *wasn't* trying to find a new mistress, then London would give Gideon the opportunity he needed to enact his original strategy – woo the mistress and encourage her to leave Thomas for him. He also couldn't deny the thrill he felt at the prospect of spending so much time with Amelia in the coming weeks.

"Well, then," Gideon lifted the crystal tumbler in his hand, "perhaps this might be the Season for me to join, as well."

Thomas's grin grew and, without a word, he reached his own glass out to touch it to Gideon's and toast their design. They spent the rest of the evening without another word on the subject, but the conversation never left Gideon's thoughts. He was impatient for the coming weeks. Because that was all it would take. Only a few more weeks, and he would have Amelia Becham.

AMELIA

"This is going to be an interesting few months," Lydia commented as she and Amelia jostled in the moving carriage.

It had been four days since she'd met the Duke of Birmingham, and in that time, Thomas had been relentless in his scheming. He'd also brought Lydia up to speed, and as far as Amelia could tell, her sister had been only too happy to assist him. So, Thomas and his staff left the day before for his Townhouse, Coventry House, and today, Amelia and Lydia were packed and following.

"I imagine so," Amelia replied.

"We haven't had much time to talk about everything, Amelia," Lydia began. "How are you feeling?"

"Truthfully, I'm not sure," Amelia confided in her. "A week ago, life was normal. I was tending the garden, bringing you soup, stitching a new design on an old dress, and now we're off to London to buy a new wardrobe, twitter about Society, and catch a duke. It's all a lot to think about when I do pause to do so. The absurdity of it all."

Lydia scowled at her. "You're not out to 'catch' anything,

Amelia. You and I both know you are not a scheming fortune-hunter or title-hunter."

"Thomas is scheming," Amelia muttered.

Lydia rolled her eyes. "Because that's Thomas. He wants you to be happy. And he's not scheming for you to marry a duke. He's scheming for you to get to know and marry the only man you've ever shown an interest in. Who, from what he tells me, showed a similar interest in you. That man just also *happens* to be a duke."

Amelia made a noncommittal noise in the back of her throat and stared out of the carriage window. So, Lydia continued.

"And why should it be absurd?"

Amelia turned back to her sister with a small, resigned sigh. "Oh, Lydia, you know it's absurd for me to marry a duke. I know Thomas doesn't think so, but you and I have better sense than that."

Amelia had wavered the past few days. Whenever she thought of seeing Gideon Edwards again and spending more time with him, she was filled with a new kind of excitement. But there was always that pernicious voice in the back of her mind that remembered this man was a peer of the realm and well outside her station. Thomas's confidence would run through her mind, as well, but it could never quite silence that little voice's incessant whispering.

"I don't see why, my darling," Lydia said soothingly, reaching out to squeeze Amelia's hand in her lap. "Would it be absurd for me to marry a titled man?"

Amelia pursed her lips and looked out at the passing countryside again, unable to meet her sister's eye as she knew exactly what Lydia was implying. And Lydia knew her response, too. Of course, it wasn't absurd for Lydia to marry a man with a title. She *would* marry a man with a title, and soon, if Amelia had anything to say about it.

Lydia, sensing her point had landed, let go of her hand,

sitting back against the cushioned seat once more. Moving on, she said, "So, tell me about him. You've yet to tell me anything about the Duke of Birmingham. What's he like?"

"I don't know him," Amelia admitted with a shrug, face still turned away.

"I know," Lydia soothed. "But what was it like when you met him? From what Thomas tells me, you clearly felt something."

Amelia thought for a moment, pulling her gaze back into the carriage as she tried to find the words. "It's more than I can explain," she told her sister, the person she trusted most in all the world. "From the moment I saw him, I was drawn to him. I've never felt anything like it before. It felt like an immediate and undeniable connection between us, and I didn't even know his name yet. More than that," she met her sister's nonjudge-mental blue eyes, finally saying the words out loud, "I feel as though…as though there was a whole part of me I had never known existed, which came to life upon meeting him and just feels right. So right that I don't know how I made sense before without it. And I had only been waiting to meet him for it to awaken. Like something in him fits with this part of me."

She shook her head, looking down, still trying to make sense when she knew she couldn't. How could she explain something so profound, so astonishing, so…*true*.

"I know," she continued, staring at her fidgeting hands in her lap. "I know it's nonsensical. I don't know him. I can't tell you the first thing about him. I spent barely an evening with him. It's absolutely foolish, but I can only describe it as… he feels like the other part of me." She felt her face heat at the ridiculousness of what she just said, but that was exactly what it felt like.

"It doesn't sound foolish in the least," Lydia said quietly, a hint of wonder in her voice. "It sounds beautiful."

Amelia looked up to meet her sister's accepting gaze, and she agreed wholeheartedly. What she felt with the Duke of Birming-ham…it *was* beautiful.

GIDEON

*G*ideon circulated the Welsey's large, stiflingly warm ballroom. It was romantically lit with hundreds of candles, and music filled each and every corner. He was surrounded by brightly and extravagantly dressed people, many of whom twirled and danced in a sea of color on the center dancefloor. He prowled the edges, weaving in and out of people, snagging a drink from the refreshment tables now and then before finishing it quickly and handing it to a passing footman as he waited.

How people enjoyed these events, he never understood. Not only was it almost unbearably hot with so many bodies crushing in on him, but the mothers and daughters trying to catch his unmarried eye pushed his tolerance to its limits. They hadn't seen him at a proper ball since he'd first returned to England six years ago, and his attendance now was bringing the wolves out to hunt.

After speaking with Thomas earlier in the week, Gideon had happily packed himself up and made his way to his Townhouse in London, leaving Genevieve in the care of her governess, Mrs. Potters. He was here for Amelia Becham, and if he had to suffer marriage and title hunters circling his bachelor blood, so be it. He was not unused to it and had perfected his cold, aloof persona over the years. He wasn't his father's son for nothing, after all.

Finally, he recognized Thomas's light blonde hair and humor filled eyes entering the ballroom. Following close behind were two very similar looking young women, one of whom stood out under his scrutiny and sent a shock of awareness across his skin, stopping his feet.

He wasn't sure if it was his singular focus on the woman joining the ball or if the rest of the room, indeed, hushed at the new arrivals, as well. He realized it was the latter when, a moment later, the buzz of whispered words took up the silence with a vengeance.

Regardless, an unmoving Gideon kept his eyes on his query, the edges of his lips pulling up for the first time that night. Her sister carried many of the same features as her, but where Thomas's mistress was at once sweetly beautiful and sensually striking, the younger Becham girl was all soft sweetness, like a pretty cherub of a woman.

As he watched the trio progress further into the ballroom towards the dancefloor and Gideon, he noticed that unlike last time, when the mistress had worn a well-loved, older style dress, tonight that lovely figure was delightfully on display in a rich, dark green silk of the most recent fashion. Gideon would have paid a small fortune to rip the stylish garment right off her.

Thomas greeted a few acquaintances and made uncomfortable introductions. After a moment, his gaze found Gideon's across the dancefloor before giving him what looked like an amused smile and nod. Gideon returned the gesture and shifted his focus back to the woman he'd come for, only to find those soft brown eyes already on him. He couldn't help his smirk as he watched the blush he was growing increasingly addicted to spread over her face.

In his periphery, he saw Thomas lead the younger Becham onto the dancefloor in a flurry of pink silk. The mistress kept her eyes locked on Gideon's, however, as if nothing existed except for him. She watched him like he was the beginning, middle, and end of her entire world.

Gideon made his way to her.

"Miss Becham," he greeted her, taking her gloved hand and placing a delicate kiss atop it. "What a pleasure to see you again."

"Your Grace," she replied, her husky voice breathless, causing his pulse to quicken even at the distasteful address. Said by this woman in that voice made him ache to hear it again. More than that – he wanted to see how far he could push it, push her, see if he could make her *scream* it. And then he'd push still further until she forgot herself completely. Until she remembered nothing but his name.

His voice came out rough with arousal when he told her, "You look lovely, my dear."

The flush on her face deepened, running down her neck to where her luscious breasts strained against the neckline of her dress. His breath caught when his eyes moved back to her face to find her smiling at him. The first smile she'd ever given him, and one he'd not soon forget. "Thank you, Your Grace. You look very handsome, as well."

He chuckled, "I'm thrilled you approve. Might this handsome gentleman have your next dance?"

She nodded, looking both confident and still nervous, and Gideon was once again struck by this woman's honest contradictions – her natural vulnerability even with her vast experience as a mistress.

He offered her his arm and led her to the dancefloor. He wasn't going to lie to himself, he was eager to pull her delicately curvy body close to his. Inappropriately close. And he did just that. It did nothing to ease his desire, though, as he led her expertly through the dance. If anything, he realized as he breathed in the warm vanilla of her perfume, holding her like this only teased him and made him crave touching her further.

"You dance well," he commented, hoping to distract his mind and body from his growing desire.

"Thank you," she said. "Thomas's mother taught me when I was young."

"Ah," he nodded, understanding. "Well, if she was indeed a mother figure to you, it seems reasonable that she would."

"I have heard Your Grace has a sister...," Amelia's voice trailed off, the question in it clear.

"Genevieve," he supplied. "She's sixteen."

"Lady Genevieve," she repeated before continuing. "Forgive my delicate question, but was she fortunate enough to have someone fill such a role for her? I believe your mother passed when she was quite young."

Gideon tried not to acknowledge the sadness that had been his lifelong companion waking up inside him. Instead, he forced himself to smile at her, knowing it probably looked more like a grimace. "Yes, our mother died when Genevieve was one. She has a young governess now, ever since I returned from abroad when she was ten and replaced most of the staff. I imagine Mrs. Potters is more of an older sister figure to her. I have hired some of the best instructors in the country, however, to teach her all the things she needs to be successful when she comes out."

He felt her squeeze his shoulder as he spun them around the ballroom, as if she could somehow sense his sadness.

"She is very dear to you." The way she said it didn't sound like a question, but he answered anyway.

"There is nothing I hold dearer." He didn't understand why, but his voice came out almost defensive. She gave his shoulder another comforting squeeze.

"How lucky for her. To have a brother who loves her so much."

Amelia's light brown eyes were warm and unassuming, and it made his chest ache. Being seen so closely. Down to the soft center where an unloved little boy still resided. He didn't like remembering that boy was there, but the way she was looking at him.... That little boy liked being seen with those eyes.

He wasn't planning on doing it, but it was those eyes on him. The way she made him feel like she understood there were feelings he kept hidden. Even from Genevieve. Even from himself. The way she didn't push further to see them herself, but just acknowledged and accepted what she saw in him.

As the dance came to an end, he went off-plan and asked, "Would you care for a stroll on the terrace, my dear?"

She gave him another trusting nod and took his arm so he could lead them out. She didn't seem to notice the whispers that followed her, seemingly only aware of him. It was a gratifying experience for Gideon.

Stepping outside, they walked in silence in the crisp, cool night air as he searched for his goal – a dark corner, which he found farther down the already empty terrace. He was aware of her every step, every breath. She did not pause or hesitate, but followed him with ease, and her implicit, instinctive trust satisfied yet another deep need within him. One that he'd never registered having before.

Reaching the shadows, he pulled her in front of him to rest her back against the stone exterior of the house. They were completely hidden from prying eyes, should anyone choose to join them outside. She said nothing, nor asked anything. She simply let him guide her and looked up at him with expectation and patience.

"You captivate me, Amy," he whispered, leaning forward, his hands on her upper arms, thumbs stroking her skin. He nestled his face into the side of her neck, inhaling her vanilla scent, letting it comfort him and the softness she had unwittingly exposed within him. He was surprised that it did not upset him, her seeing the sadness he still held inside. A part of him, *that* part of him, felt the oddest desire to show her all of it. See if she would accept it. See if it was enough for her.

He let his lips barely skim over her sensitive skin. He delighted in how she shivered in response, tilting her head to give him better access, her chest rising and falling rapidly.

Lifting his head, Gideon brought his face a hairsbreadth away from hers. "May I kiss you, my dear?" he asked, needing her permission.

He didn't remember she was a mistress. That she was with someone else. That they barely knew each other. He wanted to kiss the woman that inherently saw he had love in him. And he wanted her to want to kiss him, too.

Again, Amelia nodded her head in consent, and his chest warmed. He sealed his mouth over hers. His kiss was soft, but his grip on her arms tightened, pulling her close. Her hands moved gently to his chest, and she hesitantly matched the movements of his lips with her own.

The gentleness of the kiss left him as he became drunk on her taste, deepening the kiss. His hands moved down to her waist, pulling her still closer, while her hands wrapped around his shoulders. He bit her full bottom lip lightly, and she went lax in his arms with the sweetest moan before her kiss turned desperate and hungry.

A moment later, however, she pulled away, moving a hand to his chest to separate them.

"I am sorry, Your Grace," Amelia breathed, her voice and free hand shaking as she reached it up to touch her lips. She didn't elaborate on why she was apologizing or stopping, but understanding hit him square in the chest. She was still with Thomas. He hadn't meant to bring her out here or kiss her. He hadn't been thinking about any of that at all. He had only been feeling those emotions that were brand new to him.

They had to move delicately, he remembered, but he was still thrilled by this wonderful night with her. Their conversation. Their kiss. She kissed him like she had never been kissed before and yet would die without it.

"Not at all, my dear," he traced his fingers down her flushed cheek like he'd been wanting to since the day he met her. "I understand." He leaned forward and placed a chaste kiss on her lovely lips. Stepping back and offering her his arm again, he murmured, "Shall we?"

AMELIA

*A*melia had a later start to the morning than usual. Even with their late arrival home the night before, she found herself unable to sleep, replaying her evening with the Duke of Birmingham. The conversation, the dances, the smiles, the small touches and stolen glances, and most especially, that kiss.

The first kiss of her life, and it was absolutely perfect. Better than she could have ever imagined. And she was eager. Eager for another. Eager for what came next. Eager for the future. Because now she found herself believing as Thomas and Lydia did. The Duke of Birmingham really did want to be with her, regardless of their stations in life.

She made her way down to the dining room for breakfast. The sun shined brightly through the room's sheer curtained windows, lighting up the pale walls, and she found Thomas and Lydia already eating and whispering. She could guess about what, and she would rather they engaged in other kinds of whispering together. Although, she was happy with their progress from the previous night and how often the two had danced together.

Amelia made her way to the dish laden side table and began filling a plate as Thomas teased her, "Ah, look who's finally chosen to join us."

"Oh, stop it, Thomas," Lydia chided before turning her attention to her sister. "So," she asked, "how was your night with His Grace, then?"

They had all been tired and quiet during the carriage ride back to Coventry House, lost to their own thoughts. This morning, however, Thomas and Lydia seemed impatient to hear about Amelia's night with the duke.

Amelia took her seat on Thomas's free side, across from Lydia, and bit back her smile. "I think it went well," was all she offered.

"Well?" Lydia repeated incredulously. "Amelia, he hardly left your side all night. I'd say that went better than 'well.'" She looked to Thomas for support.

"Indeed," the teasing glint still in his eyes. "Not to mention how he whisked you away almost as soon as we arrived. Tell us, what did Gideon want to discuss out on the terrace?"

Lydia groaned, but Amelia met his eye. "What do you *think*, Thomas?"

"I imagine it wasn't your opinion on the rather lovely hydrangeas neither of you could see in the dark."

"You imagine right. And how was *your* night?" she asked with a glance between her two companions at the table.

"Oh, no, you don't—," Thomas started, but Amelia cut him off quickly.

"You two seemed to dance as much, dare I say more, than His Grace and I did."

Lydia blushed. "Well, of course, it was a ball after all."

"Hmm," Amelia let her skepticism hang in the air as she chewed her breakfast, watching Thomas's sudden solemnity with amusement. He didn't meet either of their eyes.

After a moment's pause, Amelia swallowed her bite and added a satisfied, "It seems it was a productive evening for all three of us." She was rewarded by a blush matching Lydia's come over Thomas's fair face.

Thomas met Amelia's gaze, and she gave him an encouraging smile. He cleared his throat. "Yes, I suspect I'll hear from Gideon soon enough for my permission to court you. I'd hardly be surprised if he called on you today with how attentive he was last night. And next week we have the Humphry's Garden Party and Perrington's Ball."

"Will His Grace be in attendance at both?" Lydia spared Amelia the question.

"I have no doubt. By then he'll be officially courting Amelia, as well, I'm sure."

"You're quite confident," Amelia couldn't help the trickle of doubt in her mind. The duke was clearly pursuing her, and she was beginning to trust Thomas's sense on this. And yet, she was human and that small voice couldn't resist echoing in her mind, wondering if it was all just a bit too easy.

"As should you be," Thomas replied.

"Amelia," Lydia said in her uniquely soothing manner, "everyone saw the attention His Grace paid you last night. He made no secret of it, nor does he appear the type of man to keep his intentions close to the chest. He wants to be with you as clearly as you want to be with him. He will not wait."

Amelia nodded and had faith in Lydia, Thomas, and the duke, pushing her self-doubt out of her mind.

Her doubt crept back in over the following days, however, as Lydia and Thomas's assertions did not come to pass. For three days after the Welsey's Ball, she received no visit or note from the Duke of Birmingham. As if their night together hadn't even occurred.

Amelia was sitting by the library window in the afternoon

on the third day, distracting herself with embroidering the neckline of one of her new gowns, when Thomas strode in and announced with satisfaction, "Gideon will be joining us for dinner."

Lydia glanced at him from where she reclined on the couch with a book, then her gaze snapped to Amelia's. Amelia, on the other hand, had her eyes glued to Thomas with such immense relief on her face, the satisfaction in his expression seemed to waver.

"He is?" It was Lydia who spoke, sitting up with a smile spreading on her lovely face. "He's reached out," she exclaimed to Amelia.

"Well, not quite," Thomas admitted with hesitation.

Amelia, who was torn between shocked excitement and relief, lowered her stitching to rest on her lap. "What do you mean, Thomas?" she asked calmly.

"Well, since I hadn't heard from him, I thought I'd help him on. I invited him to dinner, and he accepted," his embarrassment prevented him from meeting her eye, unwilling to watch the happy surprise leave her face as she realized Gideon wasn't, in fact, calling on her, but rather Thomas was playing matchmaker.

"Ah," was all Amelia said. She had started to consider many alternatives the past few days. Perhaps the Duke of Birmingham wasn't as serious as they'd thought him to be; he had changed his mind; he had realized the weakness of her social standing or, dare she consider, her lack of experience from her unpracticed kiss.

She felt her companion's eyes on her as she looked outside the window and absorbed the implications of Thomas's words. Their excitement dwindled as they watched the heaviness of Amelia's thoughts weigh down upon her.

Taking a deep breath through her embarrassment, doubt,

and simmering anger, she stood and gathered the gown she was working on. "I'd best get ready then," she said steadily and left the room.

If he was coming, she would keep her head high and her doubts hidden. There was nothing else for it.

GIDEON

*G*ideon had been pleasantly surprised to receive Thomas's invitation to dine at Coventry House that evening. He had been growing impatient to see Amelia Becham, the memory of how she'd looked at him when they spoke about Genevieve, her comforting gestures filling him with a strange tenderness. And then her kiss. How perfectly, innocently, sweetly she kissed – as if there had been none before him and would be none after him.

She was absolutely amazing and knew just how to fulfill his deepest needs, ones he hadn't even realized he possessed.

He hadn't known how he was going to make it the few more days to the Humphry's Garden Party when Thomas's letter arrived. Not only had he immediately accepted, he was thrilled to document yet more evidence that Thomas was ready to find himself a new mistress and was supportive of Gideon assuming his role with Amelia. Either that or Thomas did indeed hope to set Gideon up with the younger Becham girl, but he pushed that distasteful thought aside. Not even Thomas was so progressive as to think a duke could marry the sister of his friend's mistress. He'd likely been closer to the truth that the young girl was ready to enter her sister's profession, but given how often Thomas had danced with her at the Welsey's Ball, he was likely clearing the way for himself. So, Gideon chose to believe Thomas was giving him his blessing to assume responsibility for Amelia.

He arrived at Coventry House with his spirits high and was shown promptly into the drawing room, where the other dinner party attendees waited. The room and house had much the same balanced lightness and understated luxury as its country counterpart, clearly decorated by the same hand. Likely Thomas's mother. Lydia, dressed in a soft green gown, sat on a cream sofa facing the room's fireplace as Thomas stood beside her. Both of them paused their conversation as they greeted Gideon. He spared them a quick greeting before his eyes moved with impatience to the woman plaguing his every thought.

Amelia was seated separately in an armchair by the fire, wearing a deep red dress that made her soft brown eyes appear darker and Gideon's mouth go dry. Her face was neutral, her posture regal, and her body alluring. Finally, he saw what he had envisioned as the confident and proud mistress.

And Gideon could sense her displeasure.

At what, he wasn't sure. At the exclusion of her lover and sister's conversation? Was she jealous? His eyes narrowed, his possessiveness rearing up. Yes, she was still in an arrangement with Thomas, but she soon wouldn't be. She was his. She had to know that by now.

Perhaps she was displeased at Gideon's silence the past few days. That thought tasted better, but of course, she also knew he couldn't reach out to her yet. She had stopped their kiss for the exact same reason.

But if she was his, so, too, was he hers, he realized. Maybe he should have sent a letter or some word conveying such. They hadn't yet spoken plainly after all, and she didn't know of his intention to be with her with any certainty.

Whatever the reason, something in Gideon sat up, at attention, knowing it was his responsibility to fix whatever had caused her upset.

"Gideon, will you spend the *entire* evening at the door or do you plan on joining us at some point?" Thomas's voice dripped with amused sarcasm, forcing Gideon's eyes away from the most beautiful thing he'd ever seen, which currently required his attention. He still hovered in the doorway, having yet to join the party that watched him.

Both Thomas and the younger Becham sister had smiles playing on their faces, and he was certain his hope behind tonight's invitation and the bait to join them in London was correct. He gathered his focus, ready to search out a private moment with Amelia over the course of the evening and fulfill his duty to her.

"As I did accept your invitation, I might as well join you properly," Gideon quipped, stepping into the room and in Amelia's direction.

"Don't let us pull you from your examination," Thomas remarked. "Amelia does look quite ravishing tonight, doesn't she?"

Definitely correct. Thomas was handing her off to him. Wonderful. This would make things so much easier.

Gideon's eyes moved back to the woman in question as he stood before her. Her lips had thinned and face reddened, but she stared studiously into the fire, not looking at him.

Yes, she was not happy in the least.

"I have yet to see her look anything short of exquisite," he spoke honestly, his eyes never leaving her face. She looked at him then, and he saw something vulnerable and unsure shine beneath that proud exterior.

Did his silence after their kiss make her think he was abandoning her? Surely not. But why the wariness?

They needed to speak. Damn the waiting.

He stepped closer to her seat and blocked out the other two

occupants of the room who were already whispering between themselves. Amelia watched him, still quiet, still cautious.

"Would you take a turn about the room with me, my dear?" he asked softly.

She stood without a word and wrapped her arm around his. He proceeded to lead her out of hearing range of the other couple.

"You're rather quiet, Amy," he observed, his voice low as they walked around the small piano stationed in the room. "Will you not speak to me?"

"What would you like me to say, Your Grace?" she asked, her voice even, features still schooled in indifference, but those expressive eyes were turned toward the room, away from him.

Enough of that. He paused them in front of some painting of a country landscape and turned to her, angling her body towards him when she tried to face the painting.

"What's the matter?" he asked directly.

He saw the immediate denial pass over her features before she stopped it. She stared into his eyes as if searching for something, weighing something. He let her make her perusal, not balking or hiding from her investigation, letting her see and assess his unwavering resolve. He didn't know what she searched for, but after their first dance the other night, he would let her see all of him if that's what she needed to trust him. He'd let her see all of him, regardless, if he could manage it. Manage being so completely vulnerable.

Whatever answer she was looking for, she seemed to discover it because the indifference melted away from her features. Gideon was struck by the depth of insecurity that replaced it. No, more than that. She looked defeated. Maybe even lost.

"I am confused, Your Grace," she said. Her voice so soft, it was almost a whisper.

Gideon felt his chest squeeze – not just at her words, but her honesty, her forthrightness. She didn't bother lying or pretending with him. He knew, in that moment, with an intense certainty he couldn't explain, she would never lie to him. She'd lay herself bare at any question he asked. It calmed him and made him ache at the same time. Made him want to give her more. Give her the thing the sad little boy inside him wanted desperately to give to someone and have them accept it.

He didn't bother to pretend not to understand, either. Of course, he understood. "Because I kissed you and then you didn't hear from me," he supplied, his voice warm.

She simply nodded. Her vulnerability and defeat making his own vulnerability and regret more pronounced.

"And so, you thought I had second guessed myself and my feelings for you," he continued. "You thought I changed my mind. That I did not want you."

No nod this time, but he saw the confirmation written on her face.

"You're wrong," he told her simply. He saw the hope blossom in her eyes and her rein it in. Her doubt bothered him. His thumbs rubbed circles on the skin above her elbows. The warmth and spark coursing through him from where his skin met hers.

"You feel this, don't you?" Gideon asked quietly. "You feel what's between us. Somehow, we understand each other. We know each other. We are connected to each other. Before we even exchanged names, we knew we belonged to one another. I am yours, Amy. And you are mine. You feel it, do you not?"

She stared at him, shocked, but after a moment, her head dipped into a single nod of confirmation, his words pulling her out of her doubt.

"Say it," he commanded firmly, letting his dominant nature leak through his words, knowing it would reassure her.

"Yes," her voice was so, *so* soft.

"Yes, what?"

"Yes, I knew," she answered. When he said nothing, waiting, she continued, her voice firming with each word she spoke. "I knew the moment I saw you I was yours."

"What else?" he pushed.

"And I knew you were mine," she added quietly.

"If you knew that before anything else, why would you doubt it now." He put the question to her as a statement and saw his meaning settle in her mind, the last of her defeat, doubt, displeasure falling away as her eyes lightened. He felt a weight lift from his chest at the sight.

"I am sorry," he continued. "I did not reach out to you out of respect for Thomas, but I should have realized that truth, as well. I owe no explanation to anyone to be there for you, and I should have prioritized you over what I thought proper. You are mine." He dropped one hand from her arm to take hold of hers. "I will always take care of you. And I will always want you."

"Always is a terribly long time, Your Grace." He was relieved to see the teasing glint shining in her eyes but didn't miss the hope there also.

"*Always*," he repeated. "And you know that, too. Trust what you feel, Amy. Trust it, and accept it as our truth. I won't let propriety matter more than your needs, and you will trust what you feel between us."

"Always," she mocked gently, her eyes twinkling, and Gideon had to use all his willpower not to kiss her right there in front of some random painting in the Coventry House drawing room.

AMELIA

$\mathcal{A}$melia felt better than she had all week. Her conversation with the Duke of Birmingham reassured her, and it filled her with the security she'd been lacking as more days had gone by without any word from him. Now, his deep, velvet voice circled her head as they sat down to eat in the dining room.

I am yours, Amy. And you are mine.

It was a relief to know he felt the connection between them, too. She had been fairly confident he did but hadn't known for certain until now.

"So, Your Grace," Lydia started as they filled their plates with the decadently fragrant food served to them by the circling footmen. "How are you enjoying the Season thus far?"

"It's been the best yet," he replied.

"As if you've ever joined the Season before," Thomas scoffed, adding the seasoned fish to his plate.

"So, my response proves accurate," he countered.

"Would it not then also be your worst Season, Your Grace?" Amelia asked, smothering her sarcasm in sweetness as she lifted a bite to her mouth.

Gideon narrowed his eyes from the seat beside her, but his lips pulled up into a charming and amused smirk.

"An argument could be made," he acknowledged.

She swallowed her bite, glancing sidelong at him. "A rather sound one, I'd wager."

"Perhaps," and she felt a bizarre giddiness at the sound of his chuckle before he turned to his own plate and began eating. After he finished his first bite, he asked Lydia, seated across from him, "How is your first Season, Miss Lydia?"

"Much as I rather expected," she replied diplomatically, taking a sip of wine.

"And that is?" he pressed.

"Full of unkind faces and whispers," she supplied, picking up her fork and knife again. "But also lovely dresses, music, and dancing, so there is some balance."

"At least none of those unkind faces are at this table tonight," Thomas offered even as he nodded in agreement with Lydia.

Amelia noticed Gideon observing the couple seated in front of them as they ate, and she wondered if he picked up on the obvious connection between them, too. It wasn't like the one she shared with Gideon, which had been instant, confusing in its potency, and one they were still exploring and understanding. They were building a relationship around it. Thomas and Lydia, on the other hand, had a lifetime of a relationship already in place, and for them, the connection still needed to be unearthed and acknowledged from within it.

"You mentioned you ladies were quite close to the Dowager Countess of Coventry," Gideon spoke. Amelia took a pause in her eating, laying her utensils gently against the plate as she reached for her wine. "How did that start?" he asked.

"Mmm," Thomas made a slight noise indicating he would answer once he swallowed his bite, which he promptly did. "Our fathers had been friends practically their whole lives, I think. So, when my father died, it was Lydia and Amelia's father who first stepped in to care for me."

"And then when our mother also passed on," Lydia picked up the thread of Thomas's story from beside him. "Thomas's mother did the same for us."

"We were much like a set of mismatched, broken pieces that all somehow fit together as a family," Amelia explained.

"You are quite fortunate in that regard," Gideon murmured to the table, and there was a note in his voice that pulled her gaze to him.

She had noticed it the other night. There was a deep sadness in Gideon, one likely connected to the awful story Thomas had shared with her about his past. It had to be since both that night at the Welsey's Ball and tonight, they had been discussing families when she caught a glimpse of it. His sister. The Colbrook-Becham family. Perhaps he was also broken but hadn't yet found all the pieces, beyond Genevieve, of course, that fit with him.

"Your Grace's parents have also passed?" Lydia asked the obvious, and Amelia immediately wanted to kick her. If only her leg could reach under the damn table.

His voice came out hard. "They have."

"Were you not close?" Lydia asked, hearing it and tilting her head.

Gideon laughed as he made a grab for his wine. There was no humor behind the sound. "Not in the least," he replied.

"You don't need to talk about it," Amelia said to him softly. Unable to stop herself, she reached out a hand and laid it on his forearm.

Gideon's head snapped to hers, and she registered the tightness of his clenched jaw. The heaviness of his memories weighing in on him. He blinked at her, and she was relieved to see the tension leave his face and his green eyes melt as he looked at her.

"Thank you," he murmured. "I would like to tell *you*, I think. One day soon, if you will let me."

She felt her heart flutter as her chest filled with joy at what he was offering her. Intimacy. Trust. Strengthening their bond in a real, tangible way.

"I would be honored," she kept her voice low so their companions would have a more difficult time hearing what passed between her and the duke. "I am here for whatever you want to share with me, Your Grace. Whenever you're ready."

She smiled at him, and he seemed unable to return it. His proud expression masking a delicate vulnerability underneath it. She took back her hand and faced forward once more, picking up her utensils and cutting her next bite. Amelia did not acknowledge the way her brother and sister watched her and Gideon with obnoxiously pleased expressions.

"What should we expect at this garden party, then, Thomas?" Amelia calmly changed the subject.

GIDEON

*G*ideon meant it. What he said to her. He did want to tell Amelia about his parents, his family. About his father's abrasiveness and neglect. His mother's unmitigated disinterest, and his obsession with making her happy. With loving her enough. The way he ran. Ran far and fast the minute she died. His guilt at leaving his sister behind, with no one to stand between her and their miserable excuse for a father. The scared little girl he'd returned home to, who didn't speak for almost two years and watched him with dark, unfathomable eyes, unsure if she could trust him. The years he spent timidly offering that little girl his affection, similarly unsure if she would scorn it, ignore it, judge it, only to have her soak it up like a starved creature.

So, he gave her more, beginning to trust that she accepted it. And the more he gave, the more she came out of herself and began to trust him in return. He still remembered the way his heart stopped at the quiet, shy "good morning" twelve-year-old Genevieve had given him after nearly a full two years since he returned home. They were the first words she had spoken to him in her whole life.

Gideon wanted to lay all of that before Amelia. To tell her each and every little thing, every fear he had ever held. Things he'd never shared with anyone before. The scarred boy inside him nodded with something he hadn't felt for close to thirty years. *Hope.*

"If you'll excuse us, gentlemen," Lydia said as she and Amelia stood from the dinner table to retire to the drawing room. Amelia turned towards him as she rounded her chair, catching his eye and giving him a small, infinitely warm smile. Gideon had to clear his throat and shift in his seat to move past the feelings that smile stirred in him.

Once the ladies had exited the dining room and both men were served brandy and cigars, Thomas stood and rounded the table, angling Amelia's vacated seat towards Gideon before sitting in it. Gideon adjusted his own chair to face his host, laying one forearm flat on the table, cigar in hand.

"To a pleasant evening," Thomas held out his tumbler, and Gideon lifted his from the table to tap it against Thomas's. They both drank before Gideon resumed his position and Thomas continued speaking. "Where have you been, my friend?"

"I haven't been anywhere," Gideon answered truthfully.

"Allow me to rephrase since you are being intentionally obtuse," Thomas rolled his eyes. "Why haven't we heard from you since the Welsey's Ball?"

"I had not realized anyone expected to hear from me," Gideon replied, puffing on his cigar before continuing. "I admit it was foolish."

Thomas made a derisive noise in the back of his throat. "Considerably. I did not enjoy watching Amelia grow more upset with each passing day."

Gideon felt his brows pull down. Yes, he was becoming more confident with each interaction that Thomas was moving on from Amelia, but this was even more direct than Gideon anticipated.

He turned away, focusing on taking a drink of his brandy. It wasn't time yet to broach the topic with Thomas, even if the man was laying it before Gideon invitingly. Gideon and Amelia were still solidifying their connection, their relationship. That took precedence over both his and Thomas's impatience.

Placing his glass down, Gideon faced his friend again. "I understand," he acknowledged. "And I am glad to be here now."

Thomas's jovial eyes narrowed slightly, assessing him. "Yes," he responded. "And since you are, is there anything you'd like to discuss now before we rejoin the ladies?"

What in the world?

Thomas wanting to move on from Amelia was inconceivable to Gideon. How anyone moved on from such a fine woman, Gideon couldn't understand, but he wasn't going to argue that. Thomas's foolishness was Gideon's good fortune, and he'd be damned if *he* ever let her go once they were together.

But Thomas's impatience was more than he could believe. Gideon was likely a thousand times more impatient to be with Amelia. To move forward not only physically, but also in these new, intensely intimate ways he was only just starting to crave and didn't even remotely comprehend. Why was Thomas rushing this more than even Gideon?

The priority was Amelia, though. He would put her comfort and feelings above all else, including whatever the hell this was.

So, he kept his eyes on Thomas's and answered firmly, "Not tonight."

AMELIA

The evening was perfect. The dinner. Seeing Gideon and Lydia talk. His admission of what he wanted to share with her. How he wanted to let her in. Amelia lost herself in thoughts of the future. Of the closeness with Gideon. Of nights like tonight becoming a regular occurrence. Of his sister joining them. Of their two families turning into one.

She could see what it would be like when the duke joined them every week. Because his intentions for her had never been clearer. He had only been moving slowly out of respect for her brother and guardian. Thomas had gotten it in her head that Gideon would move quickly, but it seemed in this, he wanted to do things properly.

The thought warmed her.

Once they excused themselves after dinner, Amelia and Lydia made their way to the drawing room.

"Well, it seems things are better now, aren't they?" Lydia dove right into the topic as they walked. "Did His Grace explain why we didn't hear from him?"

"Yes," Amelia ducked her head so Lydia wouldn't see the

smile she was unable to hide. "He wanted to be respectful in Thomas's eyes."

Lydia scoffed loudly. "As if Thomas gives a damn about propriety."

"He probably assumed he would in this."

"We can't fault His Grace for that, I guess," Lydia put on a begrudging tone that made Amelia laugh.

"No, I guess we cannot," she agreed.

"He's probably seeking permission to court you right now," Lydia said confidently as they entered the drawing room and sat down beside each other on the sofa, facing the warmth of the fire. "This is the perfect opportunity."

"I hope so," Amelia admitted. "I feel better after speaking with him, but I would like things to be more official so I need not second guess myself so often."

Tea was brought in and set on the small table before them. Lydia leaned forward to pour them each a cup before handing one to Amelia.

"Understandably," she assured her, relaxing back with her own cup in hand. "But there's no reason for you to second guess yourself. He's just a little cautious, that's all. He's clearly serious about you. It seems all men share such caution when it comes to love." Lydia looked away, stirring her tea absentmindedly, and Amelia took the opening that finally, *finally*, presented itself.

"I take it Thomas is continuing to take his time, as well?" she asked.

"What?" Lydia's head snapped back to hers, the blush creeping up her face. "Whatever do you mean?"

"Lydia, please," Amelia rolled her eyes. "If I can be honest about the Duke of Birmingham, you can be honest about Thomas."

"There's nothing to be honest about," Lydia mumbled.

"You love him," Amelia said bluntly, lifting her cup and

taking a sip of the warm liquid. "And he loves you. Can you blame *him* for being slow in his pursuit when you're slow in even admitting it to me? I can't even begin to imagine fighting it as long as you both have."

There was a pause following Amelia's words as they both drank their tea and watched the flames crackle in the fireplace. Amelia refused to speak first.

"I don't know what's taking him so long," Lydia finally whispered, lowering her cup to rest in her lap.

Amelia wanted to jump up from her chair and cheer, but she knew that was exactly the wrong reaction. Instead, she smothered the urge with a smile and ventured, "I imagine he's experiencing the same fear you are when you consider expressing your feelings."

Lydia huffed, slouching back against the seat cushions and letting her frustration show. "But isn't that his burden to bear, not mine?"

"Why on earth does that fall to him alone?"

"Because he's the gentleman, of course. He should overcome his fear and approach first."

Amelia raised an eyebrow at her sister before leaning forward to place her teacup on the table as she spoke. "I don't think that's fair. Perhaps if you had met as strangers at a party, yes, but then this fear wouldn't be there either. Nor would he love you as he already does. Your story is different, and one of you has to take the first step. Otherwise, you'll both spend your lives in love with each other, and *only* each other, but never own to it."

"Will you give this same talk to Thomas?" Lydia replied, the petulance thick in her voice.

At that precise moment, the drawing room door opened and the subject of their conversation entered, followed by a man whose bright emerald eyes were already steadfastly fixed on Amelia.

"If you wish," she made sure to answer Lydia before losing herself to the Duke of Birmingham's attentions for what remained of the evening. "But each of you waiting for the other to make the first move helps no one, Lydia. Just think on it."

GIDEON

*G*ideon was having a hard time with the idea of leaving. The hour was growing late, and he knew it was too soon to stay as an overnight guest at Coventry House, but the evening had been so wonderful, he didn't want to leave. Amelia looked absolutely radiant as he approached where she sat on the pale couch in the drawing room after he and Thomas had finished their brandy and cigars.

The peculiar conversation in the dining room and Thomas's impatience still circled Gideon's mind. It didn't seem like Thomas was coming from a place of anger. In fact, Gideon was sure Thomas was encouraging him and was disappointed that Gideon hadn't declared anything. But Gideon knew better than to open the topic tonight.

This evening was only his third interaction with Amelia, and she was his priority. Her comfort and consent came first, and tonight felt like another unexpected breakthrough for them. From her side, as well as his. He had been able to comfort her. She was starting to trust in his ability to care for her. Even more surprisingly, however, he was starting to believe he could trust her to do the same for him. Comfort and care for him and all his broken, neglected pieces. He had never before considered such a thing possible.

No, he thought as he stepped towards her on the sofa, this was a perfect evening. Everything was progressing beyond his wildest expectations. Staying the night or discussing matters too soon with Thomas would push Amelia too far, too fast. Best to let things continue on their current course and let Amelia guide him on when and where to push. She wasn't ready for more tonight.

As she watched him stride up to her now, her light chocolate eyes sparkling in the firelight, he realized he wasn't ready for more yet either. He was impatient for everything to finally be resolved, yes, but now that he had decided he was going to open up to her, Gideon wanted that first.

And so, he knew, it was time to take his leave. His heart felt full as he sat down on Amelia's vacant side. It was a novel feeling, and one he was eager to always maintain.

"I must be off, my dear," he whispered to her, aware that her sister could hear the endearment before she subtly excused herself to join Thomas by the mantle.

"So soon?" Amelia asked, the disappointment evident in her voice if not by the slight downturn of her lips.

"I'm afraid so," he gave her a warm and understanding smile, pleased by how her thoughts mirrored his own. How aligned they were in their desires. She didn't want him to leave either. "I will see you in a few short days at the Humphry's Garden Party. You still plan on attending, do you not?" he asked, adding a note of teasing to his voice.

She sighed, her eyes dropping to the floor with feigned drama. "It seems I must. The company I wish to keep requires it."

"Is that so? Such demands this company makes of you. Parading about with the gossips in your finery."

"Oh, the gossips have thus far left me quite alone," she

commented. He'd noticed how members of the *ton* had avoided conversation with Amelia at the Welsey's Ball and the unkind looks thrown her way, which Lydia had also mentioned. He couldn't blame them, if he were being honest, but he hadn't expected Amelia to notice. He'd tried to keep her focus on him the entire night. Likely adding more fodder to their whispers, but he gave not the slightest damn about that. "And I do enjoy the finery. But I'd much rather spend my nights like tonight, in peaceful intimacy with close friends."

"As would I," he agreed, overwhelmed by a feeling of contentment as he pictured quiet evenings at home with her. Eating, reading, simply enjoying the calmness of time spent together. "We will have that soon, my dear. First, we must do this right, and then I can't imagine anything more perfect than spending the rest of my days in peaceful quiet with you."

The smile she gave him then lit up his whole soul. And he meant it. The promise of their future, her smile every day – Gideon couldn't imagine a better way to spend his life, nor could he wait for it to begin.

AMELIA

"This is far more extravagant than I expected," Amelia whispered to Thomas and Lydia as he escorted them around the Humphry's Garden Party. She eyed the decadently dressed people promenading and laughing delicately in their pale-colored dresses and coats. The dresses were stylish but more appropriate for the day compared to the silks, skirts, and rich colors she'd seen at the Welsey's Ball. The party surrounded an unnecessarily ostentatious fountain, taller than any man present. Servants circulated carrying equally decadent food that looked too pretty to eat and that would almost certainly make Amelia's stomach sick with sweetness. She felt just as overwhelmed as she had when they had entered the Welsey's ballroom, but at least she could breathe the open air here.

Had that really been only five days ago? Things were moving quickly. She had first met the duke almost two weeks ago, and in that time, they moved closer to each other with every interaction. He had yet to state his intentions to Thomas, which the latter had told Amelia and Lydia with poorly disguised annoyance after the duke's departure from Coventry House the other evening. After all their conversations, the ease with which he'd stepped into their group, his desire to share his hidden sadness with her, and his parting words, Amelia found it easy to keep the promise she'd made the Duke of Birmingham. She trusted what she knew to be true. She trusted him, too. He was approaching their relationship in the way he believed right and good. He didn't realize, or perhaps didn't want to take for granted, how unconventional Thomas was as a guardian.

"It is little wonder why you never had us attend these events before, Thomas," Lydia added in agreement as they continued to stroll around the Humphry's garden. "Or why you avoid them with such enthusiasm yourself." She eyed a cluster of young ladies watching them with indiscreet smiles and whispers.

"You get used to it," was all Thomas supplied.

"I very much doubt that," she muttered. She, too, had been irritated by the duke's slow pace, but she kept that secondary to her unwavering support of Amelia.

Amelia couldn't stop her eyes from scanning those in attendance looking for the Duke of Birmingham. It took her a few minutes before she found him already striding towards them. She felt the knot of tension ease in her chest. It wasn't that she *disliked* these events so far, but she had yet to get her bearings within them. The *ton* also seemed less than accepting of new faces. Being with the duke allowed her to get her feet beneath her and concentrate on him, rather than paying mind to anyone else.

He walked directly up to their party, his dark hair tousled attractively from the light wind, adding an almost carefree effect to his sternly handsome face. *Almost.* None looking at his beautifully chiseled features, sharp emerald eyes, and rich attire would think him carefree. He was too strong, too powerful, too overwhelming to be anything else. And it was those same qualities that wrapped her in their safety when she was with him.

Amelia drank in the sight of him as he joined their group.

"Thomas," he said with a nod before turning to her sister. "Miss Lydia, you look lovely as ever."

"Thank you, Your Grace," Lydia answered, appraising him with a greater hint of curiosity today.

"Miss Becham," his already deep voice lowered intimately as he turned to Amelia. The sound embraced her senses, making her want to sigh in relief. His bright green eyes locked onto her, and she had that recurring sense of being trapped within his gaze. Only now, she was no longer unnerved by it. Rather, she let herself belong there, caught in that sea of crystal and green.

"Your Grace," she smiled at him softly and watched his cool eyes warm in response. That also seemed to be a recurring response. One he had to her, and she absolutely loved it. Loved that her smiles made such a difference to this hard man. "It is wonderful to see you again," she told him.

"Would you care to join me in a promenade?" he asked, offering her his arm. She took it without hesitation, and he led her away from Thomas and Lydia. Amelia expected them to follow, but she turned a moment later to see they had begun to stroll in the opposite direction. Likely to give Amelia and the duke their privacy while also enjoying some of their own.

Amelia felt the duke's presence surround her. The rich material against her fingertips. The hard muscle she felt beneath it. The spiced, masculine scent. She loved that, as well. It was unique and wholly him. Deep, rich, and entirely male. It made her want to sink completely into it and breathe him into her every pore.

"I have missed you," she said quietly, basking in the comfort of being with him. And she had missed him, even if it had been only two days since she last saw him. Her time with him was always so short. She wished she could have more, and less publicly so they could build on that trust they were starting to create between them.

"I love your honesty, my dear," he replied. "Promise me you will always be this honest and never hide yourself from me."

She scoffed. "I doubt it would be possible for me to hide from you, Your Grace, even if I wanted."

"Gideon," he corrected her as they continued to walk. She noticed and appreciated that he was leading her away from the other guests so they could speak more comfortably. "And why is that?" The smirk he gave her made her heart beat faster, and she felt the flush creeping over her skin.

"Because of you," she shrugged lightly.

She saw a flash of confused amusement pass over his face before his arm slipped from beneath her hand to hold it instead. Having led them slowly away from prying eyes, he now whisked her hurriedly into a small maze built on Lord and Lady Humphry's grounds. He didn't say anything, just pulled her along as he searched. Amelia grabbed the skirts of her new pale yellow day dress and followed him willingly, giggling.

A moment later, he found a suitable spot. A small alcove built off the main path in the greenery with a stone bench nestled within it. Easy enough for passersby to miss if they weren't looking directly at it. He led her over, and she took a seat before he did the same, angling his body towards hers.

He still held her hand in his as he grinned at her, clearly having as much fun as she was. His thumb began drawing circles on her skin, igniting it in the way she was coming to expect from his touch.

"You were saying?" Gideon prompted, his eyes focused intently on her, ratcheting her heartbeat back up and amplifying the sensations already coursing through her.

"Yes," her voice came out breathy from the combined exhilaration of their hurried steps and his touch. She cleared her throat before continuing. "Because of who you are. To me, I mean." She could feel the blush darkening her skin and moving down her neck.

"And who am I to you, Amy?" His voice came out low, as if they were speaking in secrets.

"I do not know," she sighed, feeling vulnerable and safe with him. She looked off into the garden path as she continued, "But I do know you see me. All of me. Parts of me that I didn't even know existed until I met you. You exposed me, even to myself. How could I ever hide from that?"

His free hand moved to cup her chin, tilting it up and urging her to meet his eyes. She did and practically preened under the fiercely possessive look she saw in them.

"You can't," he confirmed in a rough voice before moving his hand to the back of neck and pulling her lips to his.

He kissed her like a man lost to his desire, intensifying the heat that had already been growing under her skin from his excruciatingly soft touches on her hand. She felt a moan escape her, and his hand released hers to grasp her waist and pull her against him. His tongue coaxed hers into a heated dance, and the hand at her neck squeezed. She felt all the tension in her body fall away as she turned to liquid in his hands. Soft and pliant and his.

Amelia felt that need in her blood grow. The need for him. The need for more. Her hands moved over his chest, his muscles firm under his fine clothing. Moving on instinct, she curled one hand around the rich fabric, while reaching the other up to weave her fingers in the silky strands of his hair. He deepened the kiss with a groan, and warmth pooled between her thighs in answer.

He was everything. Everything, everything, everything. His hands on her, his lips on her, his tongue against hers, his scent around her. She was overwhelmed by him, and still she craved more. She craved all of him. All that he was to consume all that she was. And she wanted to devour him in kind.

She had never felt this before. This world-ending, all-consuming need. It had begun with that first kiss and only grown. Grown and grown, her body struggling to contain it.

His lips moved down her neck to below her ear, and she tilted her head so he could nestle into her. A sharp gasp left her as he found a particularly sensitive spot.

"Your Grace." She didn't recognize her own voice, nor did she know what she was saying or why.

Lifting his head slightly, his voice was a rasping whisper in her ear. "*Gideon*," he reminded her before biting her earlobe. The whimper that left her was desperate and needy as the fire intensified in her core.

"Gideon," she breathed. It felt right to say his name. She loved the feel of it on her tongue.

"Yes, Amy?" he murmured seductively between kisses, moving down to where her neck met her shoulder. She trembled in his hands.

A set of giggles broke through her lust, and she immediately shot back, extricating herself from Gideon and putting distance between them. Her head turned to the main path just as Gideon's snapped up in the same direction. A small cluster of girls was scurrying away, their hands covering their mouths as they snickered at what they'd discovered them doing. Amelia and Gideon were so tucked away in the maze that the girls must have followed them in here.

"Oh, dear," Amelia said, turning back to him. She wasn't too upset. Yes, she would have much preferred their rendezvous to remain private, but she was far too warm and relaxed to mind the prying eyes and indiscreet giggles of some young girls. Besides, the duke, *Gideon*, had made clear time and again that she was his and he would care for her. She trusted him to remove any blemishes made to her reputation.

It was with that trust that she looked at him now. She noticed the annoyance etched onto his features as he stared after the girls. His expression was stern, mouth thin, when he finally turned back to her.

He blinked, taking in her face. Once. Twice. His gaze softened at whatever he saw there, and his voice held a small note of wonder when he eventually spoke.

"You are magnificent, Amelia."

GIDEON

*S*he *was* magnificent. Gideon hadn't meant to kiss her, or at least he hadn't consciously intended to when he led her away from the party. He wanted some privacy with her, something they had yet to truly have, after she had unexpectedly told him she missed him. Unashamed. Unrestrained in her honesty. He wasn't sure if it was a core quality of her personality or something she only possessed with him, but it was refreshing and empowering to hear her speak her thoughts so openly and without hesitation. He had never experienced that kind of honesty from anyone, nor had he imagined such a thing existed. He hadn't seen anything even remotely resembling it in his parents' volatile relationship. It gave him hope. And that extremely vulnerable and fragile part of him that kept making itself known in her presence wondered if perhaps they could have something more tender than what he had initially thought possible between them.

Now, as he observed her after those damned children had interrupted them, he couldn't imagine anyone more perfect. She was looking at him with such unmitigated trust. Without a single care or worry, as if she could depend solely on him. That kind of faith was staggering. It made him immediately want to be a better man for her. To never let her down. To never lose that look, that trust. He felt the most wonderful and powerful pressure begin to settle upon him. Like he held the most precious thing in the world.

He reached over and gently took her hand in his again as he sidled closer. "I can't either," he admitted.

"Pardon?" Her eyebrows twitched adorably in confusion.

"I can't hide from you either," he told her honestly. He released her hand to clasp both of his together as he leaned forward, elbows on his knees, and stared at the grass at their feet. Instinctively hiding his gaze from hers as he exposed himself. "There are parts of me that I've kept so deeply buried, even from myself, that are coming forward now with a new kind of desperation. Because you can see them. Those hidden parts. And they want to be seen."

There was a pause before Amelia shifted closer so that the side of her body touched his. She didn't say anything, didn't pressure him. She just silently gave him her support and waited for whatever he wanted to give.

So, that little boy gave her all.

"My father was not a kind man," he began. It was odd how it was the voice of a man that filled his ears, when he felt so much like that confused, hurt child he still kept locked up tight within himself. "He didn't harm us physically, and he left me very much alone, never talking to or acknowledging me. But he was outright cruel to my mother. For a long time, it was just us three, and I never knew any warmth from her either. I can't say it was her fault. She'd wasted away in her relationship with my father, and the woman I knew was a shell. But I loved her." He was gripping his hands together so tightly that his knuckles turned white, but Gideon couldn't feel it. "Very much. I didn't have my father's love or attention, but I was desperate, *desperate*, for hers, Amelia."

He dropped his head, shaking it. "I was convinced that if I just loved her enough, that love would be enough for her. Enough to make her happy. Enough to make up for my father's neglect. It would be enough to bring her back to life." He paused, and the voice that spoke next was hard and jaded. "It wasn't.

"By the time Genevieve came along when I was sixteen, I had long since understood that my father's disregard had so completely broken my mother, there was nothing left for me in that family. But I still couldn't leave. Not until my mother died did I finally run away. I ran away for nine years. That's how long it took for my father to finally die, and when I came back, I had to live with the consequences of my selfishness."

Amelia said nothing as he stopped to take a deep breath. His posture remained unchanged, but he lifted his head to look out over the greenery around them. She simply sat beside him with the warmth of her body pressed against his increasingly cold one.

Exhaling, he continued, "I had left Genevieve alone for nine long years with no one but that devil that sired us. In truth," he forced himself to say it. "I didn't even think of her. And when I returned, she didn't speak. It was months before she said a single word around me, and even then, not directly to me. She just watched me. All the time, like some type of scared animal.

"I fired the whole staff," his teeth ground out. "Any adult in the house that had been there and allowed her to become that fearful. But it was my fault. I am her brother. Her family. And I hadn't been there for her." His voice broke on the last word, and he stopped speaking.

"How are things between you now?" Amelia asked gently after a few moments passed in silence.

That thought made him relax a bit. He unclenched his fingers, finally sitting up and rubbing his stiff hands against his thighs as he told her, "Good, very good." He still looked out into the garden as he spoke, but he could see her watching him out of the side of his eye. "It took time, but we became close. I was careful with her, and I admit it took some time for me to trust her, too. Trust that she wouldn't reject me like our mother had. But once I realized how she soaked up the affection I gave her, I focused it all on her. And she slowly came out of that protective shell she lived in." He took a few breaths, making sure he had himself in hand.

"And the piano, as well," he added now turning to face her and meeting her soothing gaze. "The piano helped. I found her a proper instructor, and she surpassed him within weeks."

He smiled at the memory, and Amelia reflected it back at him, speaking genuinely, "She sounds exceedingly talented."

"She is," he nodded.

Her face turned sober as she looked down at his hand, reaching for it.

"Gideon," she said, her soft brown eyes meeting his again and taking his breath away for the hard strength he saw within them. "You are enough. You are *more* than enough. It was your mother's failing, not yours, that she did not see it. And your father's choices, his actions, are not your burden to bear. Neither with regard to your mother, nor your sister. I know I cannot say anything to absolve you of the guilt you carry, but I can assure you, you do so unfairly. You were a child. And you were hurt and uncared for. You did what you needed to do to heal enough and become the person that could heal your sister in turn. If you hadn't gone, if you hadn't separated from the place that harmed you all your life, you might not have become someone able to show her even the slightest amount of love, which is what it seems she needed."

Her words shot through him, and he didn't know what to do or think or feel. She wasn't judging him at all, but comforting him. The little boy inside him crumbled at the words he needed but thought he'd never hear. And the man he was didn't know what to do in this moment as he felt the turmoil and heart-broken joy burn within him.

The logic of what she said made sense, but could it really be that simple?

He couldn't speak, but his eyes held onto her steady and sure ones like the lifeline they were.

She squeezed his hand, lifting it to her lips to kiss his knuckles before she clasped her free hand around him, too. Holding their hands against her chest, she spoke with unwavering confidence, "You didn't leave her, Gideon. *You came back to her.*"

AMELIA

*A*melia was filled with rage for Gideon and the sister she had yet to meet, Genevieve. She tried to curb it, knowing that was not what Gideon needed, and he clearly, *clearly*, never had someone in his life focus on what he needed.

Their parents. Their awful, terrible parents. Amelia was torn with regard to his mother and what he'd shared. She understood it was the woman's husband that had harmed her so much, she withdrew. But Gideon was her *son*. It wasn't his fault. She had brought him into this world. Many women didn't have a choice in that either, of course, so that also flashed in Amelia's mind. She had no idea what that woman's life was like, but the picture Gideon had painted for her. The way he had loved his mother and learned likely the single most important lesson of his young life, that his love was not enough, made it hard to reason away the late duchess's indifference.

And that father. He was root of that family's cancer. He was it. He destroyed his mother, Gideon, and Genevieve. And *Gideon* felt guilty? That guilt was not his to bear. It lay solely and squarely on the man Amelia wished was turning in his grave.

She could see Gideon was struggling. She was full of anger

and sadness on his and his young sister's behalf, but she also felt pride. She was honored that he had shared his story with her, something he hadn't shared with anyone before, she knew. Something he said he kept so deeply hidden, he didn't even acknowledge it himself.

"Thank you, Gideon," she said into the silence, lowering their clasped hands to her lap. He watched her with such hope, it broke her heart still further. He looked almost desperate to believe the words she had spoken, that it wasn't his fault, that this wasn't his guilt to carry, that he was enough. Damn the people that ever made him think otherwise. Damn them all straight to hell.

She gave a tiny shake of her head, focusing on what she wanted to say to him. "Thank you for trusting me."

He looked away, almost as if the emotions were too much for him, which was likely the case. She still held his hand between both of hers, though, unwilling to let go while he was so obviously adrift.

Clearing his throat, Gideon turned back to her, and it was once again the sure, confident duke meeting her gaze. She smiled at him, accepting all the parts of him, all his needs and hopes and ways of coping.

"Like I said, my dear," he finally spoke, giving her that heart melting smirk. "I can't hide from you either."

She laughed, breaking the tension. "I am very glad to hear it. It would have made our relationship frightfully unbalanced."

"Oh, but I do like unbalanced sometimes," he murmured seductively, banishing the last of the clouds that had hung over them while he shared his burden with her.

Gideon leaned into her space, their bodies already touching from when she had moved closer to him in an attempt to provide support when he was vulnerable. His free hand came up to cup her jaw, his thumb brushing along the edge of her bottom lip.

That fast she lit up with desire for him again. Only it tore through her more potent now as the weight of his trust, her anger, their sadness served as yet more fuel for their passion. She closed her eyes and leaned into his touch, feeling his face move closer, his lips brush hers.

"And I think you like it, too," he purred before sealing his lips to hers again. The kiss was different this time. The fire and hunger were still there, but their earlier frenzied passion was gone. Now, their kiss was infused with something deeply tender, slowing the pace and pulling at her heart. Her body still responded, and she placed one of her hands on his chest as she felt her skin grow tight, the moisture gathering again between her legs.

He shifted his hand to cradle her head and gave her what she craved, tightening his grip on the back of her neck at the same moment as he deepened the kiss. She had never imagined that would be something she liked or desired until he had squeezed her nape earlier. And just like that time, the action now triggered her to turn soft and warm in his arms. Becoming vulnerable and open. All for him. Because his dominating nature brought out her yielding one. Or maybe it was her nature that brought out his. Either way, they fit one another, their needs in perfect harmony.

He pulled his head back to look down at her, and she blinked at him still soft, still trusting. Gideon grinned, his eyes glowing triumphantly while his thumb traced along the edge of her jaw. She shivered at the touch.

"Oh, yes, my dear," he crooned in his deep rumbling voice, which kept the fire kindling within her. "You most certainly like it, too."

GIDEON

*Y*et again, Gideon found himself suffocating in a crush of bodies while he waited. The Perrington's ballroom was smaller than the Welsey's, but their party was far more extravagant. The large production of flowers, and the tiered delicacies and drinks piled high atop tables surrounding the space were almost garish in their grandeur. And the guests, dressed in their silks and riches, were swept away in the excessive luxury. Gideon was no stranger to luxury, of course; his own home was a prime example of the extreme wealth and inheritance associated with his title. But where his home was comforting in its lavishness, this felt tasteless and over the top.

Or perhaps he was just tired of the whole Season and the *ton*. This was his third social event in less than that many weeks – and the *ton* was beside themselves over it. Nor had they missed where he focused his attentions during these events. The added intrigue of it was making them practically crazed. That didn't stop the mothers and daughters from continuing to pursue him, however. They were unwilling to give up the opportunity to trap the reclusive and formidable Duke of Birmingham when it was before them. Luckily, his cold stares and silent judgment were still enough to discourage them when they tried getting too close. If all went according to plan, this was the last he would have to endure them and these events.

Yesterday, he had followed his instincts and opened up to Amelia in the Humphry's garden, and he had been rewarded with her unconditional, steadfast support and acceptance. She'd seen all of him. The ugliness and guilt he kept locked away from outside eyes, and she did not balk. She was so much more than the flawless mistress he originally assumed. He thought her innate vulnerability and innocence coupled with her experience was what made her so valuable. No, there was so much more to it than that. She was a balm to his lifelong festering wounds, and now he couldn't imagine his life without that kind of trust and acceptance in it. He wouldn't be able to go without it. She knew all of him, and she didn't shame him for what he carried. In fact, she had lightened the load.

Then, there was their physical intimacy, which much to his surprise and joy, now felt secondary to him in light of how *she* had cared for *him*. Yet another novel feeling, and one he was unwilling to give up. He was thrilled by how perfect they were for each other even in their passion. Her nature to surrender was the precise match to his nature to control. It's what he needed. Her trust in him and in his ability to meet her needs.

As he paced the overly hot ballroom, still reeling from the changes in him and his expectations of their relationship, he grasped that it wasn't just Amelia's combination of innocence and allure that set her apart, or even the intense connection he'd felt from the start.

No. The truth was she filled so many parts of him that he hadn't even realized were empty. That his *life* had been empty, and now she was making it whole.

It was time. She was ready. He was ready. Thomas was beyond ready based on their conversation over brandy at

Coventry House. This one last event, and then he would pay her a visit this week before speaking with Thomas. He wanted to speak with her first, though, in private, without eyes and ears a constant stone's throw away.

His eyes finally alighted on Amelia's graceful figure standing at the edge of the dancing couples. He'd been so lost to his own reverie that he hadn't noticed her arrive. She stood alone, not noticing him tucked amongst the other guests, and watched her sister and Thomas dance with a small smile on her lips.

Gideon didn't approach her immediately. He couldn't stop himself from taking a few moments to simply drink in the sight of her, his chest swelling with all the wonderful new emotions she stirred in him. Her heart-shaped face was free from the blush that often adorned it in his presence. Her burnished gold hair was styled perfectly atop her head, and those temptress' curves were wrapped in a rich purple silk. He craved her like a man starved. Not just her body, but her kindness, her strength on behalf of others, her laughter, her thoughts.

He was still admiring her when he noticed her attention shift from the dancefloor. Looking politely to either side, she observed a group of young women standing together, chatting. She *didn't* seem to observe, however, the whispers and unkind glances thrown her way as she took a step in their direction, her intent to join them clear. Gideon felt his feet move without thinking, knowing he wouldn't make it in time to intercept her. The young women whispered more hurriedly to each other before making direct, cold eye contact with the approaching Amelia and, as one, turning and walking to the other side of the dancefloor.

Amelia halted in her tracks. He could see her shocked face absorbing the ladies' rebuff. He didn't like it, even if he understood it. He wasn't quite sure what she was thinking or what she expected – why she thought she *could* approach them. Although, when he let himself follow the thought, he realized Thomas bringing her into Society and Gideon establishing their relationship in public view were both outside propriety. Nor had she been exposed to Society enough as it was to know what was appropriate.

Gideon stepped up behind her where she still stood by the dancefloor. The shock had not yet finished morphing into confusion on her beautiful face. "Good evening, my dear," he said quickly, trying to pull her attention away from the insult she was still processing. "I find myself in need of you."

"Gideon," she said his name easily as she turned around to face him, and he loved the sound of it in that husky, feminine voice. Perhaps he was imagining it as a result of his earlier musings while waiting for her, but he thought he detected notes of tenderness in her voice when she spoke his name.

Amelia smiled at him, brushing away the insult just hurled at her. "What is it I can help you with?" she asked sweetly, amusement lighting her eyes.

"I require a dance partner," he held out his hand for hers, lifting one side of his lips in a smirk.

She sighed dramatically as she considered his outstretched hand. "If I must," she declared with false resignation as she placed her hand in his. "One does not deny the Duke of Birmingham."

He laughed. "I should hope not."

Joining the couples on the dancefloor, he pulled her body to his. His blood heated at her proximity and the feel her under his palms. He saw the blush he loved color her cheeks, and he had the oddest desire to kiss them. Her warm vanilla scent comforted him as he led her through the waltz.

"There is something I wish to discuss with you, my dear," he said after a few moments spent simply holding each other and moving with the music. "In private. I would like to call on you tomorrow, but without Thomas or your sister present."

He watched as that beautiful blush spread down to the top of her chest. Her soft brown eyes held a note of uncertainty within them as they spun across the room. "Alone? Without a chaperone?" she asked, her voice low.

He chuckled, fighting the urge to laugh outright. She, a *mistress* of two years, was worried about a chaperone? What need did she have of one? Unless she was still worried about Thomas's reaction? No, he shook the thought off. After everything from this week – Thomas's behavior, hers, their shared confidences and kisses – no, she must be speaking out of habit, understandably unused to a new relationship.

Her innocent responses never felt like a show, which was yet another thing he loved about her. He was coming to believe her ability to hold contradicting truths was simply who she was. She was a professional, but she was also sweet and pure.

He answered kindly, even as he suppressed his amusement, "Yes, my dear, without a chaperone. We must be allowed to speak freely and without the expectations of those around us."

"What is it you wish to discuss?" she probed, dancing flawlessly just as she had during the Welsey's Ball. She was exceptionally graceful in how she moved.

"I would like to have a candid conversation about our future and hear your thoughts on my proposal, free from the influence of others."

He knew Amelia was a strong woman. At first, all one could see was her exceeding gentleness, but the more he spoke with her, shared with her, the things he felt with her…. It was clear that gentleness was a profound kind of strength, the likes of which he'd never encountered before.

Gideon also sensed that she was a very giving person. Another quality of her strength. And that particular aspect likely made her more susceptible to the opinions of her loved ones. In this, in her consenting to their arrangement, he wanted that discussion between only them, and her agreement only hers.

"I understand," she assured him, the edges of her mouth pulling up. She paused, biting her lip and looking over his shoulder as she considered. "You should perhaps pay call in two days' time. I can speak to Lydia and Thomas tomorrow to give us our privacy. They could use that time alone together, as well."

So, Gideon had been right. Lydia was taking her sister's place. He mildly wondered if Thomas had been waiting for the younger girl to come of an appropriate age all along. Not that it mattered, and he let the thought wander to the back of his mind, where it was already edging.

"The staff will be there, but that is unavoidable, I am afraid. Had we been in the country, we could have met at the cottage," she scrunched her face adorably to one side in passing regret, and he pulled her closer as they danced. She hid a smile at his action before explaining, "We'd only have Mrs. Nichols and Walters to worry about there, and I could have simply given them the day off. We'll have no such luck at Coventry House."

Gideon was surprised. She had a staff of only two at her cottage? Why didn't Thomas lavish this incomparable woman with riches and staff of a hundred. It wasn't even close to what she was worth.

Amelia was watching him expectantly. So much about her distracted him.

"Two days," he agreed as the song drew to a close, and she practically beamed as they continued to stand there, agreeing without words to the next dance.

She was looking at him with such unwavering trust in those large, chocolate eyes as they waited for the music to begin again, but he also noted something else in her gaze. Something deeper that made his chest clench. The vulnerable part of him, which belonged to her and her alone, was desperate never to lose that look.

AMELIA

*L*eaving the Perrington's Ball having danced and laughed the night away with Gideon, Amelia was full of buzzing energy. Both Thomas and Lydia, however, were exhausted and leaned back in their seats as the carriage made its way to Coventry House.

Thomas had been right, after all. Gideon was not one to wait or stall when there was something he wanted. Amelia worked on maintaining a stoic expression as she kept her face turned to stare out the window at the passing night. Thomas, however, called her on it.

"What's going on, Amelia?" he asked, head resting against the carriage wall, eyes barely open as he watched her. It seemed he was too tired to even bother with his usual teasing. Lydia tilted her head towards Amelia from the seat next to her.

Amelia faced Thomas in the seat across from them and attempted to seem ignorant as she asked, "Is something going on?" Of course, she failed miserably when the smile she'd been fighting broke free across her face.

"You've always been a miserable liar," he sighed. "Just tell us."

"Very well," Amelia was smiling so widely, her teeth were on full display. "Gideon is going to propose to me in two days."

It was almost comical, and Amelia did indeed laugh, as both Thomas and Lydia sprang up in their seats as though they'd had buckets of water dumped on them.

"He is?"

"Truly?"

"What did he say?"

"Oh, Amelia, this is wonderful!"

"Amelia," Thomas's voice was firmer than she'd ever heard from him, demanding her attention. "What did he say?" he repeated.

"He said he wants to have an honest, private conversation with me to discuss our future," she recounted. "He wanted to stop by tomorrow, but I asked him to wait another day so I could speak with you tomorrow instead. You couldn't wait, though." Her chiding had no edge at all as her joy overflowed, filling each corner of the carriage.

"In private?" Lydia's sweet expression was still thrilled as her brow pinched in something like concern.

"He doesn't want us burdened by an audience."

"A chaperone is not an audience," Thomas said, his voice suddenly quite sharp.

"Thomas," Amelia held fast. "A chaperone cannot *help* but be an audience. And he knows as well as you both that I regard your opinions highly. He wants my answer to be mine and mine alone."

"It would be," Thomas insisted. "He needs to talk to me anyhow. I will still need to be present."

"Thomas, you're being mulish," Lydia rolled her eyes as the carriage jostled, adding to the effect. "You must understand that he wants to *know* her answer is only hers, even if we three know it would be."

"I am not comfortable with this," he grumbled. "Nor do I want anything indecent to happen while he visits, Amelia, do you hear me?"

"Who do you think you're speaking to in that tone, Thomas Colbrook?" Amelia bristled.

"Stop, Thomas," Lydia turned to face him fully. "This is a happy moment. One we've been anxious for. What's more, Amelia and His Grace are both decent and honorable people. It is perfectly appropriate for them to keep such an important conversation between them alone. Be happy. This is what we wanted, and it's thrilling the moment is finally at hand.

"Now, tell me, sister," she continued, twisting her body in her seat to face Amelia better in the confined space, "are you happy? You're certain you want to be with him? You've only known His Grace for a terribly short time now. Do you feel as though you know him well enough to accept him?" Lydia's tone held no judgement or worry, but rather supportive inquiry.

Amelia turned her eyes from a begrudgingly quiet Thomas, sulking with his back against his seat, to Lydia. Looking at her darling sister's open face, she was honest. "It is true we haven't known each other long, but I do feel as though I know him. I admit when we first met, there was an intense attraction and connection between us, but it's grown to so much more than that even in such a small time. He's shared a great deal with me. And he's spent time with the three of us as a group."

Her eyes shifted back to Thomas. His posture was unchanged, but his blue eyes held less ire and more curiosity. She nodded to him as she continued, "You were right. We complement each other very well. In our nature, but in other ways, too."

She turned back to Lydia to explain. "For example, one would think *our* family," she gestured between the three of them "was broken from the start, but we know that's not true. We have always been whole. Gideon's family, on the other hand, seemed whole, but it's been terribly broken. And I've understood more of who he is as a result. What he carries. How his life has shaped him. There's more to him than I ever could have realized."

"It's true," they turned to find Thomas nodding in his seat. "That was why, seeing you two together and also how you reacted to one another back in the country, it finally occurred to me how well suited you were to one another. He has a hard exterior, but I think it protects something immensely fragile within him. You, sister, may seem gentle and soft, easily influenced, but your core has always been one of steel. He can take care of you, but I meant it when I said you can heal him. You've already started. I've never seen him smile or laugh as easily as he has the more time you two have been spending together."

Amelia's gaze gentled, her previous annoyance at Thomas dissipating as she better understood what he'd said to her the day she met Gideon. He was determined to irritate her, however, as he continued, "I don't see why he never paid you a proper call, though. Or why there's a rush for an engagement now. He should spend a few weeks courting you properly instead."

"Thomas, I don't understand," Amelia said, exasperated by his lack of enthusiasm. "Did you not want Gideon to ask for my hand?"

"No, I did. I *do*. I simply want him to court you first. There is a way to these things."

"You, yourself, said your friendship is based on your mutual desire to step away from tradition," she reminded him. "And you were plenty bothered by his concern for propriety the other night."

"Yes, but not when it comes to you and not in this. And I was bothered that his sense of propriety had him taking a glacial approach to courting you, not that I didn't want him to do so properly. Why didn't he ask for your hand the other night if he is so eager? Where is his propriety now in asking to meet with you alone and unchaperoned? I am beginning to question his inten–."

Amelia cut him off. "Gideon is a good man," she was adamant. "You know he would not dare act in an untoward manner with a member of your family. You would never have encouraged or allowed his attentions if he was such a man."

"I know," Thomas conceded. "*I know*. But this does not feel right to me." He paused, taking a visibly deep breath. He shook his head before continuing, "I am not fond of this plan, Amelia, but if this is how you want to proceed, very well. I trust you. I will choose to trust him." Thomas's tone left a bit to be desired in its confidence, but Amelia decided it was the best she could get in the current circumstance.

"I am sure he plans to speak with you directly after," she said, hoping to calm the last of his apprehension.

Thomas only nodded, his mouth still pulled into a grim line.

Lydia brought the conversation back to her unanswered question. "Darling, are you happy about his proposal? Even though you are growing closer and feel like you know him, you can still take more time. As Thomas said, no one is going to rush you."

"No, I do not want more time," Amelia's voice came out quieter as she was struck by what awaited her in two days. "I am happy, Lydia. So very happy." A lump formed in her throat, making her voice thick as she finished answering.

Her sensible sister, Lydia, let out a small squeal, the likes of which Amelia hadn't heard since they were little girls, and threw her arms around her. "Then I am happy, too, Amelia," she laughed into her hair.

Amelia looked over, somewhat embarrassed after her admission, and was surprised to find the smile on Thomas's, up until now, serious face. "You really are a perfect match. I am very happy for you both. Please don't doubt that."

"I would never," she tried to hide her sniffle. "It was all your idea after all."

Lydia laughed yet again, unable to contain her joy. Amelia cleared her throat and her emotions to broach the next necessary topic.

"So, Gideon will meet me in two days at Coventry House. You two can spend that time making things official between *you*, as well. Perhaps starting with a carriage ride or picnic in the park." Her words were a suggestion, but her tone brooked no argument. Now that her future was settling with Gideon, she would see the same done for her stubborn sister and, for all intents and purposes, brother.

"What—," Thomas and Lydia both began simultaneously, but Amelia interrupted them quickly.

"I love you dearly," she continued in the same tone. "You know this. And we all, and I do mean *all*, know how you feel about each other. You have done your part in securing my future, now I am repaying you with the same courtesy. It is time for you to start being honest and to begin your life together. There has never been a more opportune time for you to nurture what's between you," she finished encouragingly.

Never had Amelia said it so directly, but she knew she had done the right thing when neither of them argued her words or tried to deny them. Rather, Lydia was suddenly riveted by the darkness outside the carriage window, her face aflame, and Thomas again wore that serious expression on his usually cheerful face.

The quiet settled around them as they made the last of their trip in silence. Amelia didn't disturb it, recognizing she had struck the match, but it was for them to let it blaze.

The carriage slowed and came to a stop in front of Coventry House. Before the door opened, however, Thomas broke the silence with a steady and sure voice. "Very well," he said, eyes on Lydia, and those two words yanked her gaze to his.

Amelia only smiled, looking between them, as the door opened next to her. She took the footman's hand and left the two lovers alone to finally begin their own story.

GIDEON

*G*ideon sat at the desk in his study, his back to the windows directly behind him. He stared unseeingly at the wood paneled wall before him. The fireplace was lit on his one side, and the comforting wall of books was on his other. He reread Amelia's note, confirming the time for their meeting tomorrow. He had never been this excited for a social call before. His skin felt jittery in anticipation of at last finalizing their arrangement. He hadn't planned through how the conversation would go tomorrow, but he was confident it would be simple and just the final step in settling what they already knew.

No, he wasn't concerned about what he would say to Amelia. He was concerned, instead, about what he needed to say to his sister. He stood to pour himself a drink as he thought it over, making his way to the small side table in the corner by the bookshelves with an array of delicate crystal decanters and tumblers atop it.

Genevieve had also sent a letter today. This one inquiring none too subtly on how the Season was progressing and if Gideon had selected a wife. She, like everyone else, was under the impression that Gideon had decided to break out of his isolation to wed. It was a reasonable conclusion, of course, and with his sister coming of age soon, having a wife to guide and oversee her would be extremely useful.

Stoppering the bottle after pouring his glass, he took a sip as he walked back to his desk chair. The liquor burned its way through his chest delightfully as he sat down. Leaning back, he cradled the crystal between both palms and continued thinking about Genevieve's inquiry.

Gideon was less inclined to take a wife now than ever before. He couldn't think of anyone except Amelia. What need did he have of a wife in the end? Someone to be miserable and unhappy with, making his home an absolute punishment in which to reside, meanwhile Amelia would be in his arms, warming his bed, caring for his heart.

His heart. That thought pulled him up short. He couldn't believe he really just thought that, but now that he acknowledged it, he couldn't deny it was the truth. The way he had exposed the bleakness he carried inside himself, his memories, his burdens, and how she had received them all with open arms. Without judgement or blame. The way his chest repeatedly clenched around her in both pain and pleasure. The ache to have her. Not just her body, but *her*. To care for her. To deserve her.

And then there was his secret hope that they might have something different from the relationships that had shaped him since childhood. Taking another drink to bolster the vulnerability he felt at that wish, he continued to reflect. He was stubborn, willfully ignorant, yes, but he wasn't stupid. Yes, he wanted, *trusted*, her to care for his heart. If he wasn't as sensible as he was, he might have even believed himself in love with her. He knew better than that, but there was no more denying that the sweet, kind, playful, beautiful Amelia Becham had claimed his heart. Withered and unused as the pitiful organ may be, it was hers. Just like the unloved boy still living inside him. Just like *him*.

What to tell Genevieve, though? He leaned forward to place his glass on the desk and pulled a blank sheet of paper forth. He would tell her the truth, to start, that he wasn't searching for a wife. He had come to London at the behest of the Earl of Coventry, who had decided to participate in the Season this year. That part was simple.

No, the difficulty was that he *wanted* to tell Genevieve about Amelia. He wanted the two women to meet. He also wanted to share what he was feeling with his sister. Something he had never done, nor ever expected *wanting* to do at all. It was Amelia. Not hiding anything from her made him want to hide less from others, too. What's more, Amelia with her welcoming, nonjudgemental, calming presence – she would do wonders for Genevieve. Perhaps even bring her further out of the shell she still often kept herself safely tucked within. Amelia was a safe space. He had no doubt she would be that for Genevieve, too. Amelia could heal her. She could heal *them*.

But how could he possibly do that, he wondered as he continued to stare at the unmarked page. There was no way he could expose his sister to any woman that provided such services. It wasn't Amelia or even her character that was in question. She was impeccable and someone his sister could only benefit from knowing. But Amelia's circumstances had led her into a profession that he could not bring in contact with Genevieve. It wasn't her. It was her occupation.

Then there was the whole living situation, which had been simple enough before. Amelia had her cottage. She would live there, he would assume responsibility for it and provide for her, and he would visit her there. But after spending some more time with her, Gideon now understood that he *always* wanted to be with her. And not just to be intimate. He wanted to talk with her, dance with her, dine with her, just sit with her.

He wanted Amelia to *live with him*. That was impossible. Absolutely and unequivocally impossible. And yet, he wanted it. There was no way he could bring that scandal into his home, though. It would make no difference to him – he was the Duke of Birmingham. It would, however, bring an unaccountable amount of scandal on Genevieve. She would be ruined, never able to find a match if he did that, and he couldn't do that to her. After selfishly abandoning her when he was young, he couldn't ruin her life further. He remembered Amelia's words in the face of the guilt he carried, but it would be some time yet before he could find the strength to let it go. Strength he would find with Amelia's support.

He could wait, he told himself, picking up his quill and dipping the tip in ink. Once Genevieve was married in the next few years, he would move Amelia in with him. In the meantime, she could stay at the cottage as originally planned and he would visit her often. Likely so often that *he* would practically be living with *her*.

No, it was best he didn't disclose anything about Amelia to Genevieve at all, as desperate as he was to do so. His responsibility to Genevieve was more important than what he wanted from his sibling.

AMELIA

$\mathcal{I}$n the days following the Perrington's Ball, Amelia felt different. The whole world felt brighter and more exhilarating. She'd never felt her life lacking before. She was perfectly happy with the life she, Lydia, and Thomas had built. Yes, she expected to one day marry, and for Thomas and Lydia to also wed, but she hadn't realized how colorless her life had been before she fell in love.

In the day and a half before Gideon's visit, Amelia rarely spent a moment without a smile on her face. Lydia and Thomas watched her with pleasure, but when they left that special day, Amelia noted they did so with their own shy excitement coloring their features.

Amelia, meanwhile, could not care less that she was about to be engaged to a duke. All that mattered was Gideon, the self-possessed man that he was, the tenderness he held within, the way he made her feel. She knew she was all that mattered to him, as well.

Thomas and Lydia gone, Amelia waited in the entryway to Coventry House. She had asked the servants to make themselves scarce today, so when Gideon arrived, she opened the door herself. Amelia did her best to control her giddy joy and pounding heart as she took in the sight of him on the doorstep, her hand still on the door she held wide for him.

"Good afternoon, dear," his smirk was both arrogant and charming, and had her lips pulling up into the largest smile her face could withstand without breaking. "Are you happy to see me?" he teased, stepping in without further invitation. He reached over her head to grab the edge of the door and push it closed. Once it clicked shut, he stepped into her space, gently taking hold of her hand and placing a soft kiss to her forehead.

"Mildly," she offered, looking up at his sparkling green eyes while her heart stuttered at his gentle show of affection. She strengthened her grasp on his hand and turned, leading him into the house and towards the drawing room.

"It's lovely to see how radiantly you shine with *mild* happiness," he commented behind her as they walked into the bright, sunny room they'd be occupying. She paused after pulling him in to shut the door behind them and then led him to the couch, before which a tea tray sat ready on the small table.

"Thank you," she said cheekily, taking a seat and finally releasing his hand to pour their tea. Gideon sat down beside her, and she felt his gaze heating the side of her face.

Amelia handed him his cup, smiling. "I am glad you are here, Gideon."

"As am I," he ran the back of his fingers along her cheek before taking the cup she offered. His demeanor sobered, and he focused on the business at hand. "To that end, you know I come here with a purpose."

"Yes." Amelia ducked her head to hide the blush brightening her face in anticipation, even though she knew he could see it. He wasn't wasting any time, and she was thrilled by it.

Gideon didn't show any signs of amusement at her reaction as she might've expected. He usually seemed to enjoy her blushes, but perhaps he was just too nervous today. Of course, she would accept him, he had to know that, but she imagined it was still nerve-wracking to ask someone to marry you.

Placing his untouched cup back on the table, he spoke with determination. "I would like you to be mine, Amelia. Permanently."

Amelia looked at him then, her brow furrowing. Was this his proposal? It didn't sound like how she imagined a proposal would, but what else could it be? Wasn't he supposed to go down on his knee, though?

"Be yours?" she queried in an attempt to confirm his meaning.

"Yes," was all he replied, his face the mask of staid purpose. Here was that determined duke she had felt beneath all the warmth and smiles he showered upon her. The solid strength she constantly felt within him and that often grounded her. His warmth and care were still there for her, but his resolve was taking priority in this discussion.

For the first time since knowing him, she didn't feel settled by it. In fact, wariness began to grip her the more she watched him. She pushed, "What exactly do you mean, Gideon?"

"I would like to become your benefactor," he answered. "I will take care of you and have you be mine. Mine and no other's for the rest of our lives."

"Benefactor?" Shock encased her like ice, protecting her hopes and dreams for as long as possible before the truth she was already understanding could properly crush them. And her.

"Yes," he said again, matter-of-factly.

"You want me," her voice was low, soft from disbelief and the reality melting through her, "to be your...your *mistress?*"

Gideon blinked, confusion layering his features. He stared at her for a moment, maybe two, and then she watched his face harden, his jaw clenching as he arrived at some sort of conclusion she didn't understand. But there was so much she didn't understand in this moment, so much she could barely begin to process, that the change in his expression did little more than register.

"Yes, Amelia," his voice was hard. "And understand this, I will not share you. You are mine. For the rest of our lives, you are mine, and I am yours."

His. Even in the muddled fog of confusion and hurt overwhelming her, she couldn't deny the truth of those words. She just couldn't believe how wrong she'd been about what being his, what having him, what their relationship meant.

He hadn't been courting her at all.

He'd been *seducing* her.

She had no words. No idea of what she should say. She had been so very, very wrong.

And so, she said nothing.

She'd thought she'd be a wife. *His wife.* But he would have her as his mistress. *His whore*, she forced herself to think the word. Because that's what she would be.

But even in her pain, she wasn't sure if she should reject his offer. He was right. They did belong to one another. And she didn't know if she could deny the opportunity to be with him in whatever way possible.

She vaguely registered Gideon's temper growing as he watched the turmoil playing out on her face. The silence stretched between them.

He finally broke it, his anger bleeding into his words as he stood abruptly. "I am leaving."

She looked up into his cold, green eyes. He had never looked at her so coldly before. She had never *felt* so cold before. Frozen and shaking from the inside out.

Tears filled her eyes without her consent. She fought them, not wanting him to see, and that only broke her heart further. Because yesterday – no, not even that long ago – an hour ago, she wouldn't have thought it possible for her to want to hide anything from him. Or that she was even capable of it. She had meant what she said to him the other day. How could she hide from the person that had finally made her feel truly herself in a way no one else had, not even her own company? Now, she wondered who she really was if that was still true, and yet he had only ever seen her as a possible mistress.

As if to further validate the struggle within her, Gideon saw the tears she valiantly tried to hide. Shock flashed across his face before he quickly replaced his mask of rage.

He turned forcefully and moved to the door. Amelia couldn't make herself move or speak. She could only watch his retreating form storm across the room as the coldness within her made her shake. Her teacup rattled quietly where she still clutched it in her lap, reminding her it was there. She couldn't even bring herself to get rid of it.

Gideon paused in the doorway about to leave. Without turning around, he spoke. "You are mine," he repeated again. A reminder. A demand. "I expect you to come to terms with it. I will give you until tomorrow to do so and to end what needs ending. I will return at this same time to finalize our arrangement."

With that, he left. And the tears finally spilled over.

GIDEON

$\mathcal{G}$ideon was livid. Disappointed. Pained. *Livid*.

He tore through the streets, pushing his horse as if the wave of his emotions would come crashing down on him the minute he slowed.

Had he misunderstood the depth of her feelings for Coventry? The strength of the bond there? The commitment she had to him? Gideon had been quite confident that Thomas was ready to move on from his mistress. Perhaps he had misread something. He played back all of their interactions as he rode. No, Amelia very much had feelings for Gideon. He was not wrong about that. Nor Thomas's encouragement for Gideon and Amelia to be together, even if his pursuit of Lydia Becham had felt less certain.

Was it Amelia then? That made more sense, and it also drove his anger to unmanageable heights. She had known Thomas all her life. Their relationship was perhaps more complicated than he realized. He had clearly been a fixture for her for as long as she could remember. Their relationship may have even been a planned arrangement since childhood. He was likely the only man she had ever known, and she had been with him for two full years now. Perhaps, even with the potency of her connection to Gideon, now that the time had come for her to end her arrangement with Thomas, she was...feeling things Gideon didn't want her to be feeling.

Gideon's blood had yet to stop pounding through his body. He arrived home and made his way inside. He went straight to his study, poured himself a drink, and tossed it back. He poured another before sitting at his desk and planting his face in his hands.

The hurt on her face. The way she had looked so lost. *The tears.* Gideon didn't realize how much that would affect him. It had taken everything in him – including relying on the simmering rage that had been boiling through him – to not take her in his arms and comfort her.

Yes, he promised to take care of her. This *was* him taking care of her. He wasn't going to coddle her when she was behaving unacceptably. What did she expect? She knew she was meant to be with him. All of their interactions and conversations made that unquestionably clear. Her fear of change, the unknown – even though she knew *him*, she didn't know an intimate relationship with anyone but Thomas. It prevented her from taking the next step with Gideon.

He leaned back, his drink back in hand. He rubbed at his face and took another swig. The liquor calmed his raging anger.

He had been harsh. Perhaps too harsh, he thought. Only in demeanor and tone, he argued with himself. His words had been perfectly acceptable. And he could make up the comfort tomorrow, when she had worked through her fear and moved forward with him.

Truthfully, he hadn't been able to control his emotions. He'd felt her rejection right in the soft center he kept open for her, and he had barricaded and defended himself the only way he knew how. He couldn't bear seeing her struggle over another man. It angered him...no. No, it *hurt* him that she was looking so deeply heartbroken over what being Gideon's meant. Losing Thomas.

Still, he knew he had been too harsh. Even though he acted in self-defense against the pain, she deserved better from him. The more he calmed down, the more that certainty destroyed any arguments against it.

It was understandable that she would have a hard time letting go. He had been all business from the start instead of broaching the conversation with warmth and support. He treated it like paperwork. Like the sale of a mare. Not a change from the only man she'd ever known to the one she was meant to be with. She never denied that she and Gideon were meant to be together or claimed she didn't want him. She had only been scared, and he had been selfish. Instead of holding her through it, he tried to protect himself by glaring at her and storming out, barking demands. He stood by those demands, but he could have consoled her. He *should* have consoled her.

Damn it, she had cried. And he hadn't held her. He left her. To cry alone. To sort through her thoughts and feelings and pain alone.

Damn it.

He had gone about this all wrong. He hadn't been prepared. He thought today's conversation would be straightforward, easy, a quick necessity for them to start their life together. And when it didn't go that way, he fell back on bad habits. Anger. Coldness.

Just like his father.

Gideon finished his glass and poured yet another. No longer thinking of only himself, he recognized how he'd failed Amelia today. He *didn't* take care of her, no matter how he sliced it. And his care should not be contingent on her behavior. She wasn't a horse. She wasn't an errant child. She deserved his very best at all times.

He would treat her better. He would shower her with

comfort and warmth and smiles tomorrow, fixing his mistake. He would make her feel secure in her decision, in her trust in him. She should be able to trust him not to lash out in defensiveness, even when his feelings were running rampant. He had a responsibility to her. She deserved no less. And he would fix this. Tomorrow.

AMELIA

*A*melia had finally composed herself since Gideon left, taking some time alone in her bedroom before Lydia and Thomas returned. She didn't know how she was going to explain today's events to them when they got back. Thomas was probably expecting Gideon to still be here, waiting to speak to him. After everything Thomas said the other night, not even taking into account how accurate he'd been, Gideon's absence wouldn't sit well with him today. One day, she'd have to tell them the truth. But that wasn't today.

No, today she would simply have to be strong. Strong enough to withstand Thomas's fury, Lydia's questions, and make a decision on what she was going to do.

But she already knew.

She couldn't stop thinking about how wrong she'd been. The past weeks of Gideon's attentions, the stolen kisses and whispered words, all of it shone differently in the light of stark reality. She felt like a fool. She was so taken away in her feelings, so caught up in falling in love with him, with Thomas's confidence, Lydia's encouragement. Of course, the Duke of Birmingham would never marry her. Who was she? Absolutely no one.

Amelia knew she was swimming in a well of self-pity, and she needed to get it under control. The sadness, the foolishness, the shame. She would pull herself together before Gideon returned tomorrow for her answer, or rather, her compliance. But until then, she would let herself mourn the lost future that had felt so bright and within her reach, but had only been a dream. She would never be anyone's wife, let alone the Duke of Birmingham's.

Hearing Lydia and Thomas enter through the front door downstairs, Amelia forced herself not to acknowledge what they were expecting to find. She slipped on a mask of hope and minor disappointment before leaving her room.

She found them both looking blissfully happy as they passed the center table in the entryway with its cheerful display of flowers. They were headed towards that dreadful drawing room. She didn't hear what they were saying before they turned towards the sound of her descending footsteps on the staircase.

Lydia was the first to spring into action. Before Amelia could make it all the way down, Lydia had bounded up to her, her face bright as the sun with excitement as she grasped Amelia's hands. Thomas was at the foot of the staircase not a moment later.

"Amelia," she exclaimed. "Oh, dearest, how did it go? Did he ask you to marry him? Did you accept?"

At this last question, Lydia turned over Amelia's left hand to examine a ring that was not there. Confusion passed swiftly across her face before she turned her bright, unworried eyes to Amelia's. She likely assumed there was a reasonable explanation for why the ring was still pending.

There must have been something off in Amelia's smile, because Lydia's own dimmed once she registered it. "I have no news yet," Amelia said, maintaining eye contact with her sister as she repeated the words she'd practiced in her bedroom before they returned. She kept her feet planted on the stairs. Her hands steady in Lydia's. "His Grace stopped by, and we shared a cup of tea and conversation. He did not stay long, but it gave us time to talk without pressure and expectation, which felt quite nice. I believe our courtship is progressing well. He plans on calling again tomorrow at the same hour, which should give you both more time alone, as well. How are you progressing?"

The words sounded rehearsed even to her own ears, as did her attempt at deflecting, which of course, did not work.

"He did not propose?" Thomas confirmed, not to be distracted. Upon Amelia's nod, he added, "Well, that explains why he isn't here, then." He looked around as if to ensure Gideon was, indeed, not hiding somewhere.

Lydia was watching her, though. She pulled her sister gently into her arms and whispered softly into her ear, "I am sorry, sister."

Amelia felt the jagged edges of her shattered heart as she pulled in a shaky breath, the back of her eyes once again burning. She forced herself to keep the tears in as she returned Lydia's hug, swallowing past the lump in her throat.

Lydia let her go when Amelia pulled away and did not comment on the emotion she noticed her sister fighting to control. Thomas, as close as they were, likely didn't notice it, but Lydia knew her as well as she knew herself. Her sister could see the sadness and disappointment hanging over her like a cloud, even if Amelia was pretending it wasn't there. But Lydia would respect her privacy and be there whenever she was ready to talk.

"All is fine," Amelia assured her. "I confess to a bit of disappointment, of course, but we haven't known each other long. What's a bit more time when we consider a lifetime together?"

She finally resumed her descent, heading towards Thomas as Lydia linked arms with her, matching her steps.

"If you're sure you're still happy," Thomas asked with a probing look as they neared.

"I am," Amelia confirmed.

"Then we shall trust your instinct," he replied. They finally joined him on the landing, and he continued, "These things do take time, and while I did expect him to propose quickly, we are still in very early days. He may still be coming to terms with his own feelings. Men do take more time in matters of the heart, especially one such as Gideon, who never planned to marry at all."

It seemed Lydia had talked to Thomas about his behavior during the carriage ride home the other night as only she could really make him act more sensibly. The irony of the change was not lost on Amelia.

"And it has only been a matter of a few weeks," Lydia added comfortingly, arms still linked with hers. "Two, to be precise."

"Exactly," Thomas nodded. "As long as he did not try anything untoward with you," he turned a questioning and serious eye to Amelia.

Perhaps he couldn't fight all his instincts for the sake of sensibility. Amelia had never appreciated that quality of her brother's more than in this moment.

"Not at all," she answered truthfully, her voice thick at Thomas's concern. "Just tea and conversation."

Satisfied, Thomas continued, "Then we shall give him his time. As you both said, you have the rest of your lives, and it has only been a few weeks."

Amelia hated lying to them, but while she had given in to her melancholy in private, she had also devised a plan. She could not, *would* not, let her choices affect Thomas and Lydia's future, as indeed it would if not handled correctly. She would first see them settled, and then tell them the truth. It would kill her, break her heart, but she would cut her ties with them, let them live untainted.

"Let's eat," Amelia turned around, directing the way to the

dining room as she tried once again to deflect the attention from her. "And you both can tell me about your afternoon."

This time, her attempt was met with bright faces and timid smiles as they remembered their afternoon together.

Yes, they would be just fine. Everything would be absolutely fine.

GIDEON

*G*ideon reined in his horse and dismounted outside of Coventry House. He could feel the regret pushing to the forefront of his mind as he remembered yet again how he had left yesterday. He would do things differently today. He was going to treat her with the warmth and kindness she deserved from him.

Stepping up to the front door, Gideon prepared to knock, but the door opened before he had the chance. Amelia stood in the doorway, her sweet face serious, heavy with emotions, and those fresh brown eyes not meeting his. She didn't say a word, just stood off to the side, waiting for him to enter.

Yes, she was still hurt. But he was here to fix it. He felt the purpose and focus settle deeply within him, and he would bring that same security to her as he was supposed to. Starting now.

"My dear," he greeted her, pitching his voice into a low, intimate tenor. He lifted one side of his lips up in his usual, relaxed smirk to lighten the weight he'd allowed to build upon her. He stepped into the house, facing her with the door still open behind her back. He cupped her face, tracing his thumb along her soft, full cheek.

Finally, she looked up, and he found those expressive, warm eyes shuttered and wary. His worry grew alongside the regret. She stepped out of his touch and closed the door. Without another word or glance in his direction, she led the way back to the drawing room. Gideon followed, undaunted by the tension and challenge she presented.

Unlike yesterday, Amelia didn't sit on the couch or pour him a ready cup of tea. Instead, the windows were drawn, throwing the usually light and open room into darkness, and a fire was lit, forcing a literal heaviness to the already emotionally charged air. He instantly felt overheated. Gideon understood without needing to ask that she'd lit the fire to fight the chill he'd left her with the day before.

As if in proof, Amelia took up a place standing directly next to the mantle with her arms wrapped around herself. Gideon took off his coat and folded it across the back of the couch, making sure the usual amused tilt to his lips remained securely in place. He then strode right up to her and placed a chaste kiss on her lips as if it was the most natural thing in the world. Stepping back, he sat on the arm of the couch, crossing his own arms, and watched her, waiting for her to warm under the heat of the fire and his control.

AMELIA

$\mathcal{A}$melia's chest ached from both the pleasure of his kiss and the loss of a relationship where he would come home to her every day and give her a simple kiss in greeting. But she wouldn't be his wife. He wouldn't come home and kiss her sweetly. He would visit her or summon her to his bed when the mood struck him and only that. She banished the fog of self-pity and focused on the smile on his handsome face. The warmth in those captivating eyes. The tenderness in how he'd touched her.

"How are you?" his beautiful voice asked.

Amelia released her arms, forcing her posture to relax. "I suppose I am well, Your Grace, in all the ways that matter. And you?"

"Much better now that I am with you," he answered. "And it's Gideon. Why are you unwell?"

He had understood her meaning perfectly. Of course, he knew what weighed on her, but he was giving her the space to share her thoughts and feelings as he hadn't yesterday. She recognized that.

"I am troubled, as you can imagine," she told him, as she

clasped her hands together. She knew he would ask, so she answered before he did, "By the proposition you left with me."

"What concerns do you have, dear?" His rasping velvet voice washed over her, strong and sure. It caused some of the tightness in her to ease. Even with the bleakness of her new reality, the choice that had never really been a choice, she immediately felt better. This was why she would be with him any way he wanted, because they had a connection that went deeper than titles, status, propriety, even lust. He anchored her. Kept her steady. And she softened him.

Unlike his frustration yesterday when she was reeling, he was trying to care of her. She could feel it in the clear control and confidence emanating from him and the way he focused it on her. Such a stark contrast to the last time he was in this room. Angry, aloof, abrupt.

She met his emerald eyes and felt more secure.

"A few," she said, her voice taking on the strength he lent her, and he smiled encouragingly. "First, you swore to take care of me for the rest of my days. What will happen when you bore of me or when my years begin to show?"

Gideon chuckled. "If only I *could* tire of you so easily, Amy. You are the most beautiful thing I've ever seen, and I doubt our years together will do anything to diminish that. But to ease your worry, should I dare to ever stray from you, you will always be looked after and provided for by me and no other. Until the very last of your days. Even after I die, I shall leave arrangements to make sure you needn't worry for what remains of your life."

His words finally broke through the ice numbing her heart, warming her where the fire failed. But as wonderful as his words were, there was also the reality of the situation. "And your wife, when you have one?" She ignored the sharp pain in her chest at the thought and forced herself to speak past it. "I am sure she would not be very accepting of a lifelong mistress or the burden of one."

"I do not intend to marry," he told her, his deep voice patient and calm. "But in the unlikely circumstance I do, my wife will have no concern over where my heart lay. I will make that clear from the start. She will have a title, money, a house to run, and children to care for."

The whirlwind of emotions that bombarded Amelia was overwhelming. On one hand, she had his heart, something he had never confessed to her before. Yet, in the same breath, he told her he'd share her dreams for her life with another woman. Nor would he be faithful to her. And why would he? She was the mistress.

All the spinning in her mind stopped at a single thought. *Children.*

"Yes, children," he said, brow furrowing slightly as he scrutinized her.

She must have muttered the word out loud.

"We can have children," he said, his face softening and arms uncrossing as he understood her desires.

"They would be bastards," Amelia said with a twist of her face, hating the word.

"Yes," he grit out as if the thought was equally as abhorrent to him. "And they would be loved and want for nothing," he vowed.

"Save a name," she whispered more to herself.

She noticed a flash of pain flit across his face at whatever he heard in her voice or perhaps the truth of her words. But he didn't say anything. What *could* he say, after all?

She turned her head to stare into the fire and allowed herself another moment to apologize to the children she had yet to bear. She would have them and damn them to a nameless future. Selfishly, she would give herself the chance to be a mother.

With a deep breath, she returned to the task at hand and the family member that existed now.

"I would ask something of you," she met his eyes with determination.

"Name it."

"I would see my sister settled respectably and in a happy home before...we begin our arrangement," she said, struggling to describe their relationship.

He nodded. "Then you will see it done."

Amelia couldn't contain her relieved sigh as he accepted her biggest concern. She still had to tell him the details of the current situation between Thomas and Lydia, but just the simple surety with which he joined her in the challenge finally eased her worry. Lydia and Thomas would be settled. Between the two of them, they'd accomplish the task easily over the next few weeks.

Gideon seemed pleased to have so obviously eased her concern. He asked, "Is there anyone in particular you'd see her wed? Perhaps someone she fancies?"

"Thomas," she replied.

Gideon blinked. "I beg your pardon?"

"Thomas," Amelia repeated. Then when Gideon continued to look confused, she added, almost in question, "Thomas Colbrook. The Earl of Coventry."

"That's not possible, my dear."

"Why not?" she demanded, her brow pinching. Lydia and Thomas loved each other, they both admitted it and knew it, and they had even started courting. It should be incredibly simple. Just a matter of hurrying them along. Amelia wanted to see her sister building the home she would never have. If anyone could secure the match quickly, it was Gideon. "It shouldn't be difficult," Amelia assured him. "They love each other dearly."

"Amy," Gideon explained in an exaggeratedly kind tone.

"Thomas would not bed you while being in love with your sister. If anything, I think he has been hoping for a similar kind of arrangement with her. And we cannot make your sister a countess or gain any sort of title. We must find her a simpler, but still happy, home."

If he'd pushed her straight into the fire, Amelia could not have been more shocked.

"Bed me," she repeated, aghast. "Thomas has never bed me. I have never been with any man." She couldn't believe she even had to utter those words. Bed her? Thomas? The man who could not be more of a brother to her, her lover? That's what Gideon thought?

Gideon went rigid, his jaw clenching. Coldness seeped into his voice as he spoke, "Indeed."

He didn't believe her. It was clear in the icy shift to his demeanor. Not only did he think she had an affair with Thomas, he thought she was lying to him about it.

Amelia's sad resignation to the whole situation finally, *finally*, turned to fury. Here she was, laying her honor, her dreams, *herself* on the line for him, to have him in any way she could, to love him and see that love watered no matter the pot it was in, and he thought she could give herself up so easily to any man? To more than one? To *Thomas*? To anyone but Gideon? Did he think he was just another man in a line of men to her? Did he not see her love? Did he not feel it?

She had put all her faith and trust into him, and yet he didn't know or understand her at all. How could she have been so perfectly mistaken in that?

Amelia dropped her hands to either side, straightened her shoulders, and announced, lifting her chin, "I believe it's time for you to leave, Your Grace."

His strength suddenly felt weak to her, so she called upon her own.

His green eyes flashed. "Not yet," he replied.

Her anger escalated. "You seem to misunderstand. It was not a request." Her voice was hard.

Gideon's anger seemed to rise, matching hers. He peeled himself off the edge of the couch with such slow, precise movements, such power radiating from him, that even in her anger, Amelia's heart stuttered. Her eyes widened as he approached her, watching her like he owned her. Like she belonged to him. As if in proof, she felt the connection she had with him go taut in her chest as he stepped closer. She was pinned, ensnared, trapped by those hard emerald eyes.

As hard as he gazed at her, the hand that reached up and cupped her cheek was indescribably gentle. She was caught between her own anger, the focused control of his eyes, and the tender caress of his fingers.

He leaned down, an inch from her face, and Amelia breathed in the spice of his scent. "Not. Yet," he repeated softly, and then his mouth was on hers. He didn't ease into it. No, he took her mouth with the same ownership his eyes had collared her with. His tongue ravished her, and a moan tore through her as she wrapped her arms around his shoulders, meeting his kiss with the ferocity of her own simmering anger, hurt, desire, and love.

GIDEON

*G*ideon was a man possessed as he kissed her. She had her arms wrapped tightly around him, her body arching into his, and she met his lips with a fervor matching his own. It was aggressive. Possessive. Demanding.

When he first arrived, he had felt such immense relief and joy as she talked through her thoughts. They were alright, he'd thought. He could still sense the sadness coating her, but he was confident he could wash it away.

And when she mentioned children with such wonder in her voice…. He couldn't deny the thought of seeing Amelia heavy with his child, or playing with a little boy the image of her, or holding a little girl with his eyes did strange things to him. He'd never wanted children before, but when he added Amelia to the picture, he felt a new kind of desperation for them. He knew deep in his bones she would make an excellent mother. A much better mother than the one he had as a child. And he hated when she called them bastards. *Hated* it. But neither could he deny it.

Then, things took a turn. At first, he was sure he'd misunderstood when she said she wanted her sister to marry Thomas.

Perhaps she meant another Thomas. What other explanation could there be? She couldn't possibly mean for her sister to marry her benefactor of the past two years. Her sister – the woman Thomas seemed determined to engage as his next mistress.

Then she lied to him. The first lie she'd ever given him. He hadn't thought it possible between them after all their shared honesty and vulnerability. And such an obvious lie at that. Everyone knew the truth. It wasn't exactly a secret. Of course, even so, it was...unsavory to speak of her old lover to her new one. He could understand that. But the lie still left a sour taste in his mouth as he finally discovered the line of her candor, appropriate as it may be.

Still, he tried – he really did try – to keep himself positive and settled during today's conversation. Kicking him out, however, broke that resolve. In truth, he had not expected it. *She* lied to *him*, and she was angry at him for not buying it? She didn't accept the monumental impossibility of her sister marrying Thomas and dared to kick him out for naming it?

It was as good a time as any to demonstrate his control. He would care for her, take responsibility for all of her, give her emotional and physical security, but he would not be tamed. He would not yield when pushed.

Now, they were wrapped up in each other, trying to devour and destroy, trying to expel each of their raging emotions.

Gideon deepened the kiss with a groan. He felt her go soft in his arms, making his already hardening length turn to steel as she let go and gave herself over to him completely. Never breaking the kiss, he turned around and walked her back until she hit the arm of the couch. Lowering his hands to the back of each thigh, he lifted her onto it and nestled between her spread legs, bringing his body flush with hers. As close as he could possibly get with the barrier of their clothes between them. She wrapped her legs around him, pulling him in even more, as she shoved her hands into his hair.

He kissed down her neck. Making his way to the tops of her breasts, Gideon ran his lips barely over her skin, causing goosebumps to rise in his wake. His nimble fingers pulled at the ties at the back of her dress. Then, his hands caught the layers of fabric at her shoulders and pulled down, freeing her from the confines of her clothing.

Gideon pulled back and beheld her beauty and utter perfection. Her dress undone; her exquisite breasts exposed, nipples pebbled and calling for attention; her skin flushed; and those soft brown eyes hooded and watching him. His anger and determination dissolved into a sea of tenderness and lust. He forgot everything but her. He groaned, bending back down to kiss her neck as he filled his hands with her full breasts, squeezing gently and running the pads of his thumbs over the soft pink nipples. He licked his way down to take each peak into his mouth one at a time, flicking his tongue and biting gently.

The sounds Amelia made almost undid him. She was panting and clinging to him like he was the air she breathed.

He inched back up to her ear as one hand continued to tease her breast, rolling her perked nipple between his fingers. His other hand wrapped around her back and pulled her harder against his cock straining between them. He bit down on her earlobe, and the deep moan that escaped her was thick with need.

"Listen to you," his voice was gravelly with his own arousal, and she trembled at the sound. Goosebumps skittered along her skin where his voice tickled her. "Panting like a whore for me."

The effect was immediate. Amelia's body went rigid in his arms.

He hesitated.

A moment passed. Another.

"Remove yourself from me," she said in a hard voice, still rough with desire.

Gideon pulled his head back, eyes wide in surprise. He didn't ask questions, just pulled his hands away from her skin and extricated himself from her limbs. He took two steps back and watched her, assessing the quick turn of events. This was a new side to her, he realized, as she quickly pulled her dress back into place, covering herself, and stood.

Head high, she strode to the door, where she stopped and turned on him. He had never seen such fury in a person's eyes, let alone his sweet, honest Amelia's soft brown ones. Then again, fury like that was nothing if not pure and honest. He realized in that moment that even when she'd had sadness, wariness, confusion, even her earlier anger in her expression, she'd always had a core of trust there, too. That trust he had been so desperate, so frantic never to lose. He felt something like terror and panic wash through him as he registered that the trust that was so vital to every single part of him was visibly absent in her gaze.

What just happened?

"I am no man's whore, Your Grace," she said, her voice a fortress built between them, "and my body will know only my husband's touch. You have used my love for you to manipulate me, and I am through permitting it. I will not be your or anyone else's *whore*."

She turned and strode from the room without a backwards glance.

Gideon stood transfixed, staring at the doorway in her wake.

It couldn't be. He couldn't have been so wrong. So unforgivably wrong.

She couldn't be a *virgin*.

AMELIA

$\mathcal{A}$melia's vision was red and blurry at the edges as she stormed upstairs to her bedroom.

She had lost the ability to think when he kissed her. Never before had he kissed her like that. It set her body on fire. Such an exquisite fire, she thought she would die in the pleasure of it. Her clothes had felt too tight, the air too heated, her blood too frenzied. Amelia's body had been alive in ways she had never experienced, and it was all because of Gideon. When her nipples hardened and strained against the bodice of her dress, he'd freed her from it, causing her core to melt. Her skin had tingled in the wake of his lips as he moved along her jaw, down her neck, over her breasts. And then when he'd bitten her…she had felt that bite right between her thighs.

She hadn't been able to recognize the needy sounds escaping her. Her whole body was overstimulated, heart hammering uncontrollably in her chest. And the need. The need for more. More, more, more. It was like nothing she had ever felt before. She needed everything. She needed *him*. She couldn't understand the need coursing through her, but she had held on to him like he was all of it. And he was. Oh, God, he was.

Then, the man she loved called her a whore.

Amelia had called herself nothing less over the past day, knowing it's what she would be, but to hear him call her that. To know that's what he thought of her.

She reached her room and slammed the door shut behind her without meaning to. Her fury was so overpowering, she couldn't stop moving as she paced along her room, wishing she could throw and break things.

Amelia had spent the last day grieving, worrying, and hurting as she planned to become Gideon's mistress. She had barely been able to sleep as her mind obsessed over the thought.

But he was manipulating her. He took her trust, her love, and he twisted it. He turned it into a weapon to make her what he wanted. And she had allowed it unquestioningly. Thinking he still cared for her. Respected her. Loved her. That it was only because of their vastly different stations in life that they were forced into such a circumstance.

Now, as she tried to force her jittery body to sit on the edge of her bed, she felt confident in her decision. At least in this moment. Maybe it was spur of the moment, maybe it was driven by emotion, maybe she'd regret it later. But right now, as she sat on her bed, hands atop it on either side, leg bouncing erratically…. Right now, she meant it.

It was one thing to love each other and be together as best they could within the rules of Society, a peer of the realm and a gentlewoman. It was something else entirely to think her a liar and a whore who slept with men for convenience and gain. For money. She was not that, had never been that, and if that's what he thought of her, then he'd never known her at all. Let alone loved her.

GIDEON

*A*fter a few moments spent paralyzed in shock, Gideon was jolted back to reality by the sound of a door slamming shut. It spurred him into action, and he grabbed his coat and stormed from Coventry House, stopping only to demand from Hughes where the earl was. He rode hard as he urgently directed his horse.

It couldn't be true, his mind reeled as he galloped through the streets of London. How could he have misunderstood everything so profoundly? He could not have made such a horrible mistake.

He needed to talk to Coventry. Immediately.

Gideon was at the park within minutes and found Thomas and the younger Becham girl laughing as they picnicked in the grass. Accompanied by a maid. A chaperone.

He was courting her.

Fuck.

With the selfish blinders pulled from his eyes, Gideon saw it as he observed them from a distance. Clear as could be. There was something deeper between Thomas and Lydia Becham that was more than just lust.

How did he miss that? How had he let himself become so single-minded in his pursuit? He'd thought he was an intelligent, observant man.

Gideon stormed up to where they sat and failed spectacularly in his attempt to appear composed as he ground out, "I am sorry, Miss Lydia. I need a private word with the Earl of Coventry. Without delay."

Thomas and Lydia stood up, clearly surprised by his abrupt arrival, their laughter dying.

"Of course, Your Grace," Lydia replied. She shared a look with Thomas – as if they had been expecting him. She was even hiding a smile. Thomas, too, had a smile pulling at his lips.

No, no, no.

Thomas's eyes were warm as he reached for Lydia's hand, squeezing it in farewell. Lydia's answering smile was blinding.

Thomas followed Gideon as he wordlessly led them away from the other occupants of the park, many of whom watched them with poorly disguised interest.

Seeing their goodbye, the intimacy, the shared looks. Amelia was right. They were in love. Gideon had missed it entirely.

Still, he fought with reality. Even though the truth was ripping through him, he held on to the hope that he hadn't been so exquisitely wrong.

"I can't say I'm surprised to see you, Gideon, but I hadn't expected such theatrics," Thomas chuckled good-naturedly as they came to stand beside a bench hidden from prying eyes and ears. "But I do admit, I understand your impatience." He smiled genuinely at Gideon.

Thomas had been expecting him? No. Dread inched coldly down Gideon's spine. He ignored it.

"What is the nature of your relationship with Amelia Becham?" Gideon asked the question eating at him since Amelia had walked out of that room. The question he desperately needed answered.

The smile froze on Thomas's face before melting away completely.

"What is it you are implying, Birmingham?" his voice was lethal. This was a version of the jovial Earl of Coventry Gideon had not yet met.

"I want to know what's between you two," Gideon fought from shouting. He couldn't wait much longer. He needed to know beyond all certainty, even if the truth was ice seeping through his veins.

Thomas's jaw clenched. "I know you would not be so foolish as to suggest anything immoral between me and the woman that has been my sister, and I her brother, all our lives. And as her guardian, I will not take well to or tolerate anything but the most honorable and gracious opinions of my ward."

The answer and warning were clear. Gideon's knees finally buckled under the weight of his shock and actions. He fell ungracefully onto the bench and held his head in his hands.

Thomas stood over Gideon and eyed him with suspicion. "What did you do, Birmingham?"

Gideon heard it in the low tone of his voice. Thomas would kill him if he had done anything dishonorable or disrespectful. It wasn't even a question.

Gideon lifted his head and looked at his friend's unforgiving face, feeling helpless in a way he couldn't remember feeling since he was a child. Seeing and correctly interpreting Thomas's expression, Gideon stood quickly, remembering himself and finally realizing who was before him. He wasn't talking to Amelia's benefactor. He was in conversation with her guardian.

"Nothing, Thomas," Gideon said, assuming his normal control and confidence. It sounded thin, even to his own ears. "You have failed the Becham women, however. You have not noticed what they say about them and your relationship with them these past years."

Thomas's brow furrowed, but his anger did not soften. "What are you talking about? Speak plainly, Gideon."

"The entire *ton* says Amelia is your mistress." Someone had to tell him. Thomas needed to know. In fact, Gideon was waking up to a few shades of anger, himself. Some directed at Thomas for missing the mark on Amelia's character so completely while he assumed her care.

"What?" Thomas almost yelled, the surprise driving him to take a step back.

"You heard me," Gideon said and moved in the direction of his waiting horse before either of their extreme emotions erupted on each other by mistake. "It's time to fix this, Coventry. You are her guardian, and you've allowed her reputation to be sullied under your care. I will expect you at my house tomorrow so we can start cleaning this up."

Gideon took two steps, but before he could fully make his exit, Thomas's chilling voice stopped him.

"There is a simple way to clear this up, Your Grace," he hissed. "You could marry her."

Gideon's hands clenched painfully into fists as time stopped. He stood there with his back to Thomas, feeling unable and unsure. Thomas was right, he was absolutely right. And yet, Gideon couldn't unclench his hands. Couldn't move his body to turn back. Couldn't force his mouth to ask Thomas the question he'd clearly been expecting from him.

The guilt that had been chasing him since Amelia left him came crashing down. The depths of his mistake and his treatment of her descending fully.

And still, he did not move.

After a heavy, smothering pause, Gideon forced his leadened feet forward. And left.

AMELIA

*A*melia steeled herself as she made her way down to breakfast. After three days of locking herself in her room, not joining meals, asking for privacy whenever Lydia and Thomas knocked, she finally fought through the onslaught of her grief and anger enough to compose herself. She had to come out. She also knew she had to move on with her life. Move on from Gideon, what he thought of her, how he wanted her. She needed to pick up the pieces and go back to her world before he had been in it. And if that wasn't possible, she had to continue in this one, where she knew he existed, but was not in her life.

She still felt like she had done the right thing. Her anger was still fresh days afterwards. But the sorrow was moving once again to the forefront, too. She had felt safe with him. Seen. Their connection and match felt pure and true. She had trusted him completely to be her foundation, solid and sure. Now alone, she would once again hold herself up, even if the ground felt soft without him.

Stepping into the dining room, she found Lydia and Thomas already seated and eating.

"Good morning," Amelia greeted them.

"Amelia," Lydia exclaimed, rushing over and pulling her sister into a tight gripped hug. Amelia blinked past the tears that came instinctively to her eyes. She had not actually cried in the days since rejecting Gideon, determined not to shed another tear for her broken dreams. But now in her sister's arms, she felt her throat tighten and the pressure build behind her eyes.

Thomas and Lydia had been so supportive to her these past days. They didn't begrudge her need to be alone or pressure her to come out. They each simply knocked on her bedroom door once a day to ask after her and see if she needed anything before giving her space. They knew her nature. They had lived together their whole lives. They knew she needed time. Anyone would. And they would be there for her however she needed, just as she always was for them. Just as all three of them had been raised to be.

Still wrapped in Lydia's embrace, Amelia looked over her shoulder to Thomas. His expression was serious and knowing. "I'm glad you're here," he told her.

"Me, too" Lydia agreed, pulling back but keeping her grip on Amelia's shoulders.

Amelia cleared her throat and blinked the tears back from her eyes. "I am sorry to have kept myself away for so long. I just needed a bit of time to feel like myself again. I am better now, though," she assured them. "So, tell me, what has been going on while I've been acting the hermit?" she tried to joke, but it fell flat.

"We want to know the same, actually," Lydia replied, smiling, but the heaviness of her eyes told Amelia she knew everything. Giving her sister a kiss on the cheek, Lydia resumed her seat and continued, "Come, let's eat and catch each other up."

Amelia moved to the side table and made herself a plate before joining them.

Thomas cleared his throat and spoke first. "I guess we may as well get right to it. I want us to stay in London and you,

Amelia, to continue with the Season. Birmingham was not a suitable match after all, but there are plenty of men that are. We'll also use this time to plan and hold the wedding. Lydia won't be going back to the cottage when we return to the country, and if you want to stay at the Estate with us, you know it is your home, too."

"Thomas, you're being dictatorial," Lydia commented.

"The wedding?" Amelia repeated, holding her fork in the air halfway to her mouth as she bypassed everything else Thomas had laid down and zeroed in on the announcement. Her eyes shot to Lydia, who was blushing and smiling in happy embarrassment. "You're engaged?" Amelia very nearly screeched.

"That was what you expected, no?" Thomas challenged.

She dropped the fork on her plate and shot up from her seat. She laughed, "Why did you not tell me?" The heavy clouds that hung on Amelia the past few days dispersed immediately. She pulled Thomas into her arms where he sat and then rounded the table to do the same with Lydia. The tears from before came back fresh and spilled over with her joy. "You should have screamed it through the damned door the minute it happened." She wasn't sure if she was scolding them with how full of happiness and laughter she and her words were. "I would have been out that very minute, mess and all. I am so happy for you."

She sat back down, still laughing in her happiness, one hand clutching her chest while the other wiped her cheeks. She felt teary and breathless.

"We knew you needed space, Amelia," Lydia's eyes were gentle and understanding, even as her expression was full of happiness. "We weren't going to take that from you."

"For heaven's sake," it felt good to roll her eyes, and her words still came out on a happy laugh. "Regardless, that didn't take long at all. It hasn't even been a full week since I forced you two to pull your heads out of the sand. Are you happy? Both of you? Truly?" Her eyes bounced between them.

"Yes, we are," Lydia was beaming. She reached her hand out towards Thomas, and he took it, smiling at her with such love and wonder, Amelia's chest almost burst from finally seeing it out in the open.

"Tell me everything," Amelia picked her fork back up, still smiling so much her cheeks were beginning to hurt. "When are you thinking to have the wedding? We need to get started on the planning."

Thomas answered before Lydia could, letting go of her hand and pivoting to face Amelia on his other side. "Did you hear anything else I said?"

Amelia pursed her lips. "Of course, I did. I'm not deaf, Thomas. You want me to find a husband," she reached for her tea and took a generous swallow.

"Do you want to talk about His Grace, Amelia?" Lydia asked quietly.

"What is there to say?" Amelia felt her chest ripple in pain, but she put her cup down with a steady hand. Anger was still the primary emotion within her, and she spoke with a hardness to her voice and eyes. "He thought I was a mistress for hire and wanted to employ me. I set him straight and on his way. That's the beginning and end of it."

Thomas went rigid in the corner of her eye.

"I should have killed him," he spoke harshly.

"Don't be daft," Amelia scoffed, forcing herself to behave normally about the whole situation. "You can't kill a peer of the realm."

"I can if he questions your honor," he fought to control his voice.

"Amelia," Lydia continued in the same soothing manner, balancing out Thomas's brutishness as she leaned forward. "There's more to it than that. You loved him. You still do."

Amelia took a deep breath, focusing on her plate and compiling another bite on her fork. "I do, but it does not matter.

What matters is he had one vision for our relationship, and I had another. I am willing to continue the Season, Thomas," she turned to him. "I hear there are some false assumptions circulating about what you and I are to each other. I'd like to set that straight, as well as set them straight about you two." She nodded at Lydia before lifting her fork and continuing to eat.

"I would, as well," Thomas unclenched. "I've recently learned of that apparent longstanding rumor and have been soliciting the staff's help in rectifying it. They've set to work on getting the truth circulating in various households, but we do need to do our part by attending events, announcing the wedding, and allowing suitors to court you."

Amelia did not want, nor was she ready, to enter into any courtships. She knew, though, that it was not only necessary to dispel the rumors, but also a part of moving on from everything that had happened. So, she said, "Then, let's do our part."

"Amelia," Lydia knew her sister. "Are you sure?"

"Yes," Amelia gave her a reassuring smile, still moving through the motions of having breakfast. "Now, back to you two."

Thomas and Lydia looked at each other with such undiluted love that Amelia was ashamed to admit a stab of jealousy flared in her momentarily. She was thrilled, beyond thrilled for them. But in another world, Gideon would have been at this table with them, all laughing together, sharing their own story of a proposal, and planning two weddings instead of one.

She brushed the fantasy quickly away before either of them noted her. "When are we having the wedding?" she asked again.

"We were thinking next month," Lydia turned back to her. "We can plan it as we continue to attend the various social events. Then, we'll end our participation this Season next month with the wedding before returning home. From there, Thomas and I will leave for a short honeymoon. You would have to return to the country with us, of course, as you cannot stay in London alone. We could also delay the honeymoon and finish the full Season first before leaving if you'd rather. What do you think?"

"Next month is brilliant," Amelia answered. "Rather fast, but considering the rumors already circulating about the three of us, what does talk about a quick wedding matter? And you deserve a honeymoon right away. I am rather finished with this Season, as well, if I'm being honest."

"Precisely our thought," Thomas chimed in.

Amelia was glad she had finally left her room this morning. Talking with them, laughing, being open about the insults Gideon had hurled at her and making light of them, fixing them. She felt more like herself than she had since Perrington's Ball. It felt like months had passed since then, not a mere week. So much had changed over these few short days, but this, the three of them, that had not. She doubted it ever truly would.

"Will you move to the Coventry Estate after the wedding? You could shift your belongings while we're away or wait until we return so we can move both you and Lydia at once," Thomas looped back to the final unaddressed item from his initial proclamation in a hopeful voice. "I don't like the idea of you alone at the cottage."

"Certainly not," Amelia replied. "Three is a crowd."

"Not with us," Thomas argued.

"You two will be newly married."

"That won't matter," Lydia offered.

"It won't help the rumors we're trying to squash if the alleged ward and previously assumed mistress moves in with the newlywed couple."

There was a pause as the truth of that sank in. "Damn them and their rumors," Thomas spat. "I don't want you alone at the cottage."

"Thomas," Lydia voiced what they all knew. "She makes a valid point. All this effort setting everyone right.... It would keep the rumors fresh in everyone's minds and invite further stories to spread."

"I will be fine," Amelia assured him. "I won't be alone. Walters and Mrs. Nichols will be there. And once you both are done honeymooning and are ready to have a guest, I will keep visiting. You both will come to the cottage often, too, I'm sure. We've lived with two of our trio at the cottage for years. This will be the same. Just two of us will be at the Estate, instead."

Amelia felt the impending change weigh down in the room, and Thomas and Lydia grow heavy, perhaps with guilt. But she wasn't worried. In this, she was light. She had expected this, hoped for it. This change, of all the changes the past few weeks had brought, this change was beautiful. And it gave her hope. Hope that the part of her that was sad and lost without Gideon's solid presence would be fine, just as she'd vowed.

GIDEON

"Gideon, what are you doing here?" Genevieve looked up from the book she was reading in the library of Birmingham Estate. "I wasn't expecting you home for some weeks yet. You didn't mention anything in your letter."

Mrs. Potters quietly stood and excused herself from beside Genevieve with a small curtsy to Gideon. He strode further into the comforting room with its three walls covered fully in floor to high-ceilinged bookshelves and rolling ladders. The only break in the rows of books were the two large windows on one wall and the door on the wall opposite. The fourth wall near where Genevieve sat held a fireplace with a crackling fire and an array of beautiful paintings.

Gideon approached his sister and took Mrs. Potters's vacated seat next to her.

"I'm just here for a day or two," he told her, leaning back and trying to appear nonchalant. "I came to see how you were faring."

"I think a letter would have sufficed to that end," Genevieve eyed him suspiciously. He withstood her scrutiny, not particularly enjoying how her silent, critical observations felt like she could see through the lies he layered on thickly – mostly for his own sake.

"Are you alright, Gideon?" she finally asked, closing her book and leaning forward to place it on the table while still keeping her eyes on him.

"Yes, why do you ask?"

She paused before answering matter-of-factly, "Because you're not. What's wrong?"

A maid interrupted them at that moment, bringing in tea for the returned duke without either of them having called for it. His household was pleased to see him. He, too, was relieved to be home, but he couldn't deny how ill at ease he also felt. As if he shouldn't be here. He was too far. From Amelia.

Gideon couldn't go near her, though. He needed to push through and get used to this feeling until it left him entirely.

Once they were alone, Genevieve poured two cups of tea, handing him one before leaning back with her own. She took a sip before pushing again. "Tell me, Gideon. You came back all this way because something is wrong."

"It's not anything you need to concern yourself with, Genevieve," he sipped from his own cup, avoiding her eye.

She was right, of course, though he wouldn't admit it. He came back here to see her. For himself. It was the only thing he could think of that would help him feel better, even remotely.

"I am your sister, Gideon," her voice took on a fraught quality at the edges, forcing him to look at her. "Please let me be here for you."

He assessed her and understood what she was asking. With his absence and their parents' interference, they were never given the opportunity to rely on each other as siblings might. As Amelia and her sister did. As Amelia and *Thomas* did. Because he finally recognized that relationship for what it actually was instead of what was convenient for him.

He swallowed. He missed Amelia. And envied her relationships with her family.

But maybe he and Genevieve could still have that. Or their own version of it. It was just them now. No one else clouding it with their hatred and neglect. Rejecting their love because it wasn't enough. They could be their own people. Figure out who they were. Figure out what their family looked and felt like from now on.

"You're so young, though," he voiced his argument with himself out loud.

Genevieve scoffed in a particularly unladylike manner. "Well, while I may not meet the age requirement one needs to function as a sister, let's give it a try, shall we? See if I can somehow manage it at my tender, tender age."

He rolled his eyes, and it felt good. He enjoyed seeing her sarcastic side, giving him a hard time. It had taken significant time after he'd returned from his travels for her to let out that part of her personality, and she still only did so sparingly.

Gideon had done the right thing, coming to see her. Maybe she was right. Maybe he'd feel even better if he talked to her.

Sighing, he set down his tea and said, "I made a right mess of things."

Genevieve didn't say anything when he paused, just looked at him expectantly. Encouragingly. So, he continued while she sipped from her cup.

"There is a woman," he pushed past the blockage in his throat. "I hurt her. Very deeply. I tried…." He adjusted his seat to distract himself from the shame. He didn't want to share that shame with Genevieve. His sister, who had been failed time and again. He didn't want her to know she had a failure for a brother, too.

Still, she kept silent when he didn't continue. She just waited, which prompted him to finish his thought.

He rubbed one hand over his face, not meeting her eyes as he confessed, "I tried to be with her in only the way that suited me. I vowed I would take care of her, and then I disregarded her completely for my own stubborn beliefs and selfish desires." He shook his head, remembering, before he leaned forward to prop his elbows on his knees and hold his head in his hands. He continued, speaking to the floor, "I made her less. I disrespected her. I insulted her. I took what the gossips said about her and believed it, even with all the evidence to the contrary that was before me."

He paused, forcing his head out of his hands and clasping them under his chin. "All because it was convenient. It served my needs. I...." Taking a deep breath, he said the difficult thing that no one else would understand except his sister. "I became like our father."

Gideon dropped his clasped hands from his face, letting them fall between his knees as he hung his head. He waited for Genevieve's judgement. Her hatred.

"And now?" was all she asked.

He paused, shaking his head. Taking a deep breath, he sat up and fell back against the dark green, cushioned seat.

"Now, nothing," he admitted, staring at the bookshelves opposite him and still avoiding his sister's gaze. The disappointment and loathing he'd find there. He could see her watching him out of the corner of his eye, her tea forgotten in her lap. He continued, "I'm doing everything I can to fix her reputation, which has worked easily enough. A few well-placed and well-circulated conversations, the help of the staff, the use of my own influence. It all put everything straight quickly enough. Her guardian is also doing his part, which should put the last of the rumors safely to bed for good."

"What about *you and her*, Gideon?" Genevieve clarified, her voice somewhat sharper.

"There is no me and her," he ground out.

"You love her." It was a statement.

He shook his head. "I don't believe in love."

"It's not that you don't believe in love. You've just never seen it before," Genevieve corrected him. "That's also why you can't identify it in yourself."

"That's not —."

"Do you love me?" she cut him off.

"What?" His head turned to her automatically. "Of course, I do," he answered.

He couldn't find the disgust he was expecting anywhere in her gaze. No, she only raised her eyebrow and pushed, "But you don't believe in love. How can you love me if you don't believe in it?"

"That's different. You are my sister."

She gave a pensive nod, finally leaning forward to discard her cup on the small table. "You know, our father didn't believe in love," she spoke thoughtfully, hands clasped in her lap. "He didn't love our mother, you, or me. We were his family. His children. And all of us withered under that disbelief. Mother died. You left. I retreated into myself. And yet, with him and his disregard gone, you and I have been..." she gave a delicate shrug. "Well, maybe not thriving yet, but we've been rebuilding. And somehow, you love me. Having never seen it before or 'believed' in it, as you say, you still somehow feel it for me. And I for you. And things are getting better for us because of it.

"If you truly didn't believe in love, sister or not, I don't think you would love me. Our father didn't, and I was his daughter. You were his son. I do not think you disbelieve in love. I think you're scared of it. Of it not being enough. Because it wasn't enough for father to love you back. Or for mother to care for you or live. We both know what it looks and feels like to be near someone who doesn't believe or have an ounce of love in them. That's not you, brother. I think you love deeply. Deeper than you can manage. And I think you're terrified it still won't be enough. But it is. It is for me. And I am sure it is for her."

His chest hollowed out as he looked away unseeingly into the library. He was still that little boy, unsure and confused, pulling out pieces of himself over and over and over, hoping for a smile from his heartbroken mother. Maybe one more piece, maybe the right piece, maybe just a little more, and she would be happy. She would smile. She would light up his whole world. He just had to give her some more. More of his love. His energy. Himself.

Amelia had seen that little boy. He'd shown him to her. All the broken, rotten, scarred pieces of who he still was. And she had embraced him. Of course, Genevieve was right. Amelia had already shown him his affections were enough. *He* was enough, exactly how he was.

Genevieve, his sixteen-year-old sister, wasn't done destroying him with a wisdom she shouldn't have been forced to possess at such a young age.

"You haven't become our father, Gideon. Not yet. You are allowed to make mistakes. Terrible, heartbreaking mistakes. You are allowed to be imperfect. But it's the choice you make next that matters. Will you make it right? And I don't mean her reputation. Will you bring my sister-in-law home and love her? Allow her to love you? Allow us to be the family we never had? Or will you let her heart stay broken until you both wither under the disbelief you're forcing upon yourself?"

Gideon said nothing. He *couldn't* say anything. He didn't know.

"It's your *choice*, Gideon," her voice was comforting and strong. "You can choose to be him. Or you can choose not to. Choose to be different. The way you chose to love me."

AMELIA

melia and Lydia were shown into the Dunhill's drawing room, where several ladies were already gathered. The room was sunny and floral scented from the many lovely arrangements decorating the tables along the walls. It was slightly smaller than the drawing room at Coventry House, but still splendidly decorated with expensive furnishings, bright matching colors, and an oddly welcoming feel. Like a park brought indoors.

"This is quite new," Lydia whispered quietly before Daphne Lucas, the Countess of Dunhill, rushed over to them, a huge smile splitting her face. She looked genuinely pleased to see them, which was surprising since they'd been in London for weeks and hadn't received a single invitation from her or any of the other ladies present to join them for tea. In fact, Amelia wasn't sure the countess had ever even passed a greeting to either her or Lydia before.

Even so, they were here now, and that was progress. Amelia did understand the *ton*'s past resistance in light of the rumors she now knew. Still, a part of her was a bit…well, bitter.

"Welcome, my dears," Lady Dunhill sang, "It is so wonderful of you to join us. Come in, let me introduce you to my daughter."

"It is our pleasure, Lady Dunhill," Lydia replied with a cool smile. She was a bit less understanding of Society's shifting opinions of the Bechams.

The countess's demeanor was polite and friendly, and Amelia didn't sense anything insincere in it. She gave their hostess a kind smile in return and followed her towards a pair of ladies sitting at one of the windows in the room, apart from the older women in attendance seated at the couches in the center. They looked to be generally around Amelia and Lydia's ages, perhaps a little younger.

"This is my daughter, Lady Anna," Lady Dunhill indicated a soft beauty with red hair and light blue eyes, "and her good friend, Miss Emily Davenport." Her hand moved to her daughter's companion, another pretty young lady with brown hair and caramel eyes. "Girls, let me introduce Miss Amelia Becham and Miss Lydia Becham."

They greeted each other, and the Bechams took up seats beside the ladies as the countess went back to join her other guests.

"It's wonderful to meet you properly," Anna said tactfully. Like her mother, Amelia didn't detect anything disingenuous in her tone.

"It is," Emily agreed, somehow sounding much more enthusiastic than her friend even in those two little words. "Once we learned of the awful error surrounding your family, we were absolutely mortified."

Amelia felt her face begin to flush. This was the first time anyone had directly spoken about the false rumors. Up until now, everyone seemed content to pretend the rumors hadn't existed and they were only now meeting the Becham sisters for the first time. Amelia felt herself warm to these two young women. She appreciated their candor and authenticity.

Before Amelia could think of a good reply, however, Lydia spoke, her sweet voice slightly scathing, "As were we."

"I am glad things were put to rights," Anna spoke. She was graceful and managed to maintain genuine warmth in her polite replies. "No one deserves to have wicked things said about them, and for no other reason than Society enjoying the drama and not bothering to learn the truth. I hope past misunderstandings have not harmed our friendship before we could even establish it?" The question in her words and their sincerity rang clear.

"Yes," Emily agreed, and she leaned forward and clasped Amelia's hand where it rested in her lap. Her lovely golden eyes held Amelia's gaze as if to emphasize her earnestness. "We are sorry, Miss Becham. For the dreadful things that were said about your family, for believing them, and for not gaining your acquaintance in spite of them. If you would allow us, we would like to offer you and your sister our friendship." She nodded to Lydia.

The shock on her sister's face made Amelia smile. Lydia had been holding such a grudge with the *ton*, and having any members of it be so forthright seemed to fluster her.

Amelia shifted her focus back to Emily and looked between her and Anna. She covered Emily's hand with her free one. "We would be honored," she told them. "And please, call me Amelia."

For the first time in the week since breaking things off with Gideon, Amelia felt a true wave of warmth envelope her. She was looking forward to getting to know and building a friendship with Anna and Emily.

"As would we, Amelia," Anna said, giving her a lovely smile.

Emily was positively beaming when she leaned back, cupping her tea with both hands once again, and continued excitedly, "Now, shall we discuss this Earl of Coventry and the love he has for Miss Lydia?"

The mischief sparkled in Emily's gaze as she looked between the Becham sisters. Lydia's bright red face, Emily's playful disregard for her discomfort, and Anna's pursed lips but obvious curiosity made Amelia's chest start to bubble. Before she knew it, she was laughing.

GIDEON

*G*ideon sat at the desk in his Townhouse's study, refusing to let thoughts of Amelia overcome him as he tried to focus on the letter from his Estate manager. One his Tenant's needed a little extra support right now. It was a welcome distraction, though he disliked any of his Tenant's struggling. He was just pulling out a sheet of paper to direct his Estate manager on the different provisions they should make to support the man and his family when the door to the study opened and his butler, Lewis, showed Thomas into the room.

"The Earl of Coventry," Lewis announced before leaving the two men alone.

"Thomas," Gideon muttered, turning back to the correspondence he still needed to compose. "Pour yourself a drink, I just need a moment."

"Take your time," Thomas replied, but Gideon was already absorbed in the instructions he was drafting.

Once finished, Gideon looked up to find his guest reclining on the couch, drink in hand.

"So," Gideon stood and joined him after pouring a drink of his own. He sat opposite his friend, or at least, he hoped they were still friends. So far, their conversations had focused on clearing the rumors. He wasn't sure if he'd still have a friend at the end of all this. "What brings you here this afternoon?"

"The pleasure of your company."

"Bullshit," the word came out fast and sarcastic.

Thomas made a noise somewhere between a laugh and scoff. "You are right. I came to tell you that Lydia and I are getting married."

"I knew that," Gideon told him.

"You did? It hasn't been properly announced yet. We've only told Amelia...?" The implied question hung heavy in the air.

"I surmised it from what I saw in the park the other week," Gideon told him, taking a drink of his liquor and avoiding answering Thomas's question directly.

No, he hadn't talked to Amelia. And he hated himself for it. For putting them in this situation. For how he treated her. What he tried to make her. And now for keeping them apart even as Genevieve's words constantly replayed in his mind.

"You need to make the announcement," Gideon ignored his thoughts and was direct with Thomas. "It seems we've been successful in making your guardianship clear to the *ton*, but once you announce and hold the wedding, I am sure the rumors will finally disappear for good, even from memory. You'll make her your sister in truth," he couldn't bring himself to say her name, "and that will dispel the last of it. No one would ever think to suggest, even in private, anything dishonorable of the Earl of Coventry's family."

"I know," Thomas nodded, and Gideon lifted the glass to his mouth to burn away the pain left behind from talking about Amelia. "We are planning to announce it in the coming days. I thought you did not know, however, and wanted to tell you first."

That surprised him. Thomas was being considerate and thoughtful, as if he, too, was hoping they could maintain their

friendship after all of this was over. If Gideon was understanding him – though he no longer trusted himself after all the
total misunderstandings he'd arrived at these past weeks –
Thomas was here cobbling their friendship back together.

Still, Gideon wouldn't make assumptions anymore. He was
just going to take this at face value and leave it at that.

"Thank you," he said sincerely. "And I offer you both my
congratulations."

Thomas smiled. There was a slight pause, and Gideon made
his own attempt at cobbling.

"Would you like to stay for dinner?" he asked.

"No," Thomas said, and Gideon felt a twinge of disappointment, which he quickly masked. "Thank you. I must be going
actually." He finished the rest of his drink and set the glass on
the table before standing. "The ladies are waiting for me.
They've thrown themselves quite enthusiastically into wedding
planning, and I am sure they have plenty to bombard me with
during dinner."

The envy surprised Gideon, and he was struck by how
lonely his evening, his life, felt compared to the picture Thomas
painted. He wouldn't have the laughter and love he'd witnessed
between Thomas and the Bechams. He had Genevieve, but
soon, she would marry and leave him. It would just be him.
Alone and miserable. Which was no more than he deserved.

AMELIA

"The Viscount of St. Alsbrook is here to call on Miss Becham, My Lord," Hughes announced.

Thomas was working at the desk in the library, while Lydia and Amelia sat by the window debating different patterns Amelia could embroider onto Lydia's wedding dress. They had picked it up the day before from the dressmaker, and much of the other planning for the wedding had also been falling into place. They had simultaneously continued attending social events, including the Dunhill's tea, and people had finally stopped snubbing the Bechams. Apart from their new friends, Anna and Emily, the newfound friendliness of the *ton* didn't sit well with Amelia, Lydia, or Thomas. Their judgment turned to kindness based on the hot air currently circulating. But the three of them suffered it. Playing their part, and fortunately making two new friends along the way.

Amelia let her dance card fill up at these events. Pretending the man she loved was not there, at the edges of each one, dancing with no one. Pretending she couldn't feel his eyes on her. Pretending her heart was not a broken mess trailing at his feet.

This was the first caller she had received, though. Philip Mason, the Viscount of St. Alsbrook, had danced with her twice last night. During the second dance, she was sure her face was on fire from the relentless heat of the Duke of Birmingham's gaze scorching her, but she didn't look at him to confirm what she could feel. She didn't need to. Because dance after dance, promenade after promenade, smile after smile, she could still feel him. Still feel the connection to him. If anything, the cord felt tighter, more constricting, the more she ignored it.

Lydia looked to Amelia. Amelia looked to Thomas. Thomas looked back at Hughes.

"Please show him to the drawing room, Hughes," Thomas said. "And have tea brought up."

"Yes, My Lord," Hughes nodded his exit.

"Thomas," Amelia's voice was thick. He turned to her, but Amelia couldn't find the words. She felt Lydia reach out and squeeze her hand where she was still holding the many sketches they'd been perusing and adjusting.

"It's just tea," her sister said quietly.

Thomas didn't break eye contact with her, though. He was waiting for Amelia to decide. His hope was evident on his face, even though he was trying to hide it. She knew he wouldn't force her to meet with the viscount if she did not want to.

Amelia looked away first, clearing her throat to dislodge her panic. "Not another peer of the realm," she joked instead of saying what she had actually wanted to. "Where are all the barristers and tradesmen?"

"You may just have to suffer a title, sister," he teased, but the tone did not match his grave expression.

She stood, putting aside the designs and trying to hide her shaking hands. "He is a nice enough gentleman to forgive it momentarily, I suppose. Let's not keep him waiting. Lydia?"

"Do you want me to join you?" Thomas asked as Lydia stood,

linking her arms with Amelia in support and moving towards the door.

"Not right now," Amelia forced her shoulders back, donning the politely friendly mask she'd been relying on over the past week and a half. She just had to get through it. All of it, this tea, the weeks until the wedding, and then she would be back home. Back to real life. Alone, in her little cottage, trying to forget the Duke of Birmingham existed somewhere not with her.

"I can come in half an hour to see him out," Thomas offered instead.

Amelia smiled gratefully, and then she and Lydia left the library.

"It will be fine," Lydia whispered as they walked. "Just one cup of tea, a little conversation, and then he'll be gone."

Lydia understood without Amelia having to say it. She wasn't planning on entering into any courtships or marrying, even if that was Thomas's goal. Amelia was ready for this awful Season to be over and done with. Her first and last.

"I know," Amelia said. "I can manage. He really is a kind man."

The Viscount of St. Alsbrook was standing by the window when they entered the drawing room. Amelia tried not to recall the other man that had visited her in this room. And what they did at the end of that sofa.

"Miss Becham," the viscount crossed the room, taking her hand and giving it a kiss before turning to Lydia. "Miss Lydia."

"Lord St. Alsbrook, welcome," Lydia said. "We've called for some tea. Would you please be seated while we wait?"

"Yes, thank you," he extended his arm to Amelia and led her to that godforsaken couch. Lydia went to sit by the window the viscount had just vacated.

He was a handsome man. With dark blonde hair a touch lighter than Amelia's own, blue eyes, and gently masculine features, he made many a woman look twice. And Amelia had been honest when she told Lydia he was a kind man. He was, and it felt genuine to Amelia. Not the forced, fake friendliness with which the other members of the *ton* now greeted her.

"You look lovely today, Miss Becham," he said to her as they sat down.

"Thank you, My Lord," she answered. "How did you find your ride here?"

"Pleasant. It is a good day for riding," he told her as the tea was brought in. "I would have asked to take you for a carriage ride, but thought you might be more comfortable in your own home today."

"That was very thoughtful," she said honestly. "Perhaps we can take that ride another time." Amelia wanted to kick herself as soon as the words left her mouth. She was being polite, finding it difficult to face such consideration and shun it, but she didn't want to encourage him.

"That would be delightful," he smiled warmly, a dimple peeking through on the left side. It was charming.

"And how has your day been, Miss Becham?" he asked, taking a sip of tea.

"Quite nice, actually," she told him, her hands cradling her own cup. It was easy to talk to him. "We are preparing for my sister and the Earl of Coventry's wedding. We were trying to decide on a design for her gown when you arrived."

"Did the dressmakers not design it for her?" He sounded genuinely interested in what she was sharing, even though they were discussing dresses and designs.

"Yes, of course. But at the risk of sounding too self-important, I am quite skilled at embroidery, and Lydia has asked me to make her a special design for her wedding day."

"It isn't self-important to be aware of one's strengths." He really did have a warm voice. Like melted honey. "That's kind of you to make for her."

"It's not kindness," Amelia corrected him, lifting her cup. "I am honored to do it."

"Of course," he smiled. "Do you enjoy embroidery then?"

"Very much," Amelia admitted. "We learned many things from the Dowager Countess of Coventry, but I fell in love with the creativity and beauty of needlepoint. I also find it quiets my mind as nothing else does. It's a very peaceful exercise."

"That sounds quite wonderful."

"Do you have any such pastimes?" she asked him, curious.

"Hmm," he paused to consider. "Riding, actually. There is a path near my country home, and riding there brings me the serenity you describe."

Amelia gave a small smile in acknowledgement. It was nice to talk to the viscount. He felt like he would make a pleasant friend.

That was it, though. Amelia had known that before she entered this room, as they moved through their conversation, and as they said their goodbyes and Thomas walked the Viscount of St. Alsbrook out.

Because Gideon had always been right. She had never doubted it, nor did their separation change the truth of it.

She was his and could never be anyone else's.

GIDEON

*G*ideon followed Hughes to Thomas's study, pretending he had no interest in his surroundings. But his eyes still roamed, searching out the woman he knew was hidden somewhere in this same house.

It wasn't the first time these past weeks that they'd shared space, of course. In fact, Gideon was still obliged to attend the same events of the Season for her, all with increasing wretchedness. He kept his distance, not speaking to or acknowledging her, but Thomas and Gideon had worked tirelessly to set the world right when it came to its opinion of Miss Amelia Becham. A big piece of that plan included Gideon's own word and influence. Through it all, though, he'd had to watch her circulate, socialize, dance, and smile with men that were not him. And she'd been careful, too. Avoiding him, not sparing him a single glance, as if he were just another table or piece of furniture.

"The Duke of Birmingham, My Lord," Hughes announced him before promptly leaving.

"Gideon," Thomas greeted him with a smile, standing from his desk and gesturing towards the seating area next to the fireplace before he made his way to the corner side table to pour them both brandies. Like every other room he'd seen in this house, this too was bright and friendly with pale, tastefully expensive furnishings. "Thank you for accepting my invitation."

Thomas, ever the kind-hearted and happy man that he was, had fully moved past Gideon's misunderstanding, though they were both careful not to mention the relationship between Gideon and Amelia, pretending instead that nothing had existed there at all. Gideon couldn't explain the hollowness that left in him.

"Thomas." Gideon took the offered drink and seated himself. "Will your fiancé be joining us?" he asked when what he really wanted to know was if his fiancé's sister would be joining them. The woman who knew his deepest truths. Who haunted the edges of his every thought.

He wasn't sure if he felt disappointment or relief when Thomas answered, eyeing him with knowing curiosity, "No, she and Amelia have gone shopping for the wedding."

"I see," he cleared his throat and continued his uncaring pretense. "And how is the wedding planning coming?"

"Quite well," Thomas's contented smile filled Gideon with burning jealousy. He was happy for his friend, truly, for both unselfish and selfish reasons. Gideon was glad Thomas was marrying a woman he loved. And he was more than a little relieved – surprisingly so – that Thomas had never shared any intimacies with Amelia. But in his misery, Gideon envied a smile like that and the obvious feeling behind it.

Thomas continued, "You'll stay here, yes, during the festivities? I already told the staff you would."

"Then I will," Gideon nodded. In his perfected game of pretend and avoidance, he didn't comment on how close that would put him to the woman he refused to acknowledge, even in his own mind.

"Very good," Thomas said before taking another drink. He continued in a more serious voice, "Now, I'm sure you are aware, as good as it always is to see you, I have asked you here for a specific reason. I won't insult you by being indirect. I believe you care for Amelia, especially considering the lengths you have been willing to go for her reputation these past weeks. I wish you to share a bit more on your depth of concern for her and your intentions."

"I have no intentions," Gideon ignored the hammering of his heart and bitterness coating his mouth. Genevieve's words screamed in his mind. "I admit to a fondness for her, but I do not plan to pursue a future, or even a present, with her."

He knew Genevieve was right. That he had a choice here. But for some reason he couldn't comprehend – or perhaps hadn't really tried to comprehend – he couldn't let go of what his parents had left him with. He couldn't...he couldn't make that different choice.

"No future at all?" Thomas was skeptical. As much as Gideon attempted to fool himself that his reactions and demeanor were in his usual manner, Thomas saw through the façade.

"None," he answered sharply. "You know I do not intend to take a wife."

"Yes, but I wondered, seeing the strength of your connection with Amelia, if your thoughts on matrimony had finally changed and if you might finally walk to the alter a more willing man."

"I have experienced no such change," Gideon said with finality, ignoring Thomas's disappointed expression before him and Genevieve's in his mind's eye.

"Well, then, I guess that settles it." Thomas leaned back against the cushions of his seat, taking another sip of his drink. "I will speak to Amelia today."

"What do you mean? About what?" Gideon's attention snapped up, releasing his defensiveness.

"The Viscount of St. Alsbrook."

Gideon felt his hackles rise. The Viscount of St. Alsbrook. The whelp of a man that had spent too many dances with Amelia in his arms or promenades in her company. Gideon had taken note of him – far more than he cared to admit. He had also taken the liberty to look into the man and found he had means and was generally liked by most people. Gideon, however, loathed the bastard. He refused to admit why.

"What about St. Alsbrook?" His words came out clipped.

"He has been courting Amelia and asked for my permission to offer her marriage. I know she has feelings for you, however, and I wondered if they might be mutual. If they had been, I would not have disturbed her with his request."

"Have you given him an answer yet?" Gideon was having trouble thinking through the roaring in his head. A hole was ripping itself wider and wider in his chest. The pain of it made him grit his teeth. He was sure he was shaking.

"Not yet. I think he's a decent match for her, though. They could live a comfortable life together, but I wouldn't dream of giving him an answer without speaking to her first." Thomas scoffed darkly as he imagined the consequences of doing just that.

"Indeed," was all Gideon could manage in answer. He was having trouble breathing. He needed to leave. He needed to run and rage and tear the world apart like he was being torn apart from the inside out. He shot to his feet. "Well, I must be off, Thomas. If there's nothing else?"

"There isn't." Thomas's mind was already elsewhere, likely considering his upcoming conversations with Amelia and St. Alsbrook. "Thank you for coming, my friend, and for your candor."

Gideon merely nodded and showed himself out, not waiting for Hughes to escort him. The heartbreak was violent within him. His feelings were too much for company or propriety. And with each passing moment, he was feeling more and more as though he was willingly losing a dream for the sake of holding on to a nightmare.

AMELIA

"*I*'ve had a visit from the Viscount of St. Alsbrook,"
Thomas announced as he, Lydia, and Amelia sat for
a cup of tea in the drawing room after dinner.

Amelia took a fortifying sip. Thomas had been clear that he
wanted her to find a husband this Season. She knew it wasn't so
much about ridding himself of her burden, but more a personal
apology for the false hope he'd given her around the Duke of
Birmingham. He was worried for her and wanted her happy
after her heartbreak. She, on the other hand, had gone along
with the Season for the purpose of clearing her name, deciding
to deal with any offers if and when they came. If she was being
honest, she hadn't thought she was capable of getting any, especially after her experience with the duke.

The viscount was a nice man. He had paid her compliments
and calls. He asked about her life and interests. He made her
smile, even if she hadn't laughed. Thomas liked him. Lydia
seemed less enthusiastic, but accepting overall. And yet, Amelia
did not want to marry him. She appreciated his friendship and
attentions, especially as a new, deep loneliness was taking root
within her. But she still loved Gideon. That wouldn't go away

any time soon. How could she marry the viscount when he was only a distraction from the hole left over from losing the man that completed her?

The truth was as the days and weeks built up, so too did her doubt and growing regret for rejecting Gideon. How could she blame him for believing those rumors about her and pursuing her accordingly? The memories had been real. The time they'd spent together. Their conversations. Their feelings and passion. None of that had been false. And if those rumors were so well-known about her, which it seemed they had been, it was absolutely appropriate for him not to marry her. Yes, as he got to know her and saw her with Thomas and Lydia, a part of her argued that he should have noticed the nature of their relationships, seen that something was amiss in his understanding. But if he was so sure those rumors were the truth, how *could* he have noticed it?

And now that her anger had cooled and she set about living her life without him, she was left with nothing but grief and loss. She missed him. She missed talking to him. Joking and laughing with him. Feeling the weight and focus of his eyes. The joy of his smiles.

Who gave a damn if she was his mistress or his wife as long as they were together? But then she would think of Thomas and Lydia, and she could not bring such scandal on them when they were just about to embark on a happy life together.

"What did he want, Thomas?" Lydia asked, bringing Amelia back to the moment when she didn't fill the silence.

"My permission," he answered, not looking away from Amelia.

Again, the silence was loud and unending. Thomas broke it. "I haven't given him an answer," he shared. "He is a good man, and he will take care of you. But I will not force you into anything. I want your happiness, and if you will not find that with Philip, then I do not want you to marry him. It is your decision."

"I do not want to marry him," she told him.

He forced a note of cheerfulness into his voice, "Then you won't."

Yet, again the silence weighed down upon the room, each consumed with the heaviness of her answer. Thomas with his disappointment. Amelia with her heartache. And Lydia with the understanding that her sister intended never to marry. She would spend her days devoted to a man she was separated from.

Lydia set down her cup. "Amelia, I'm getting a bit tired. Would you help me sort through the packages we bought today before retiring?"

"Of course," Amelia shook off her melancholy, setting her teacup on the table, and focused on her sister.

The ladies bid Thomas goodnight and made their way to Lydia's bedroom. When they reached the landing, however, Lydia looped her arm through Amelia's and led her instead to the latter's room.

"What's going on?" Amelia asked as her sister steered her in the wrong direction.

Lydia didn't answer. Instead, she ushered Amelia into her own bedroom and closed the door behind them. "I wanted to talk to you privately," she said once they were alone and closed off from stray ears.

"About what?" Amelia's voice came out defeated. She knew Lydia wanted to continue the conversation about the viscount, and Amelia didn't know how to explain it to her in a way she'd understand. She was still Gideon's. She always would be. There was no husband for her out there.

"I want you to accept the Duke of Birmingham," Lydia stated decidedly.

Amelia physically reeled, taking a step back once she registered what Lydia said. She had already been mentally preparing her excuses for rejecting the viscount, when her sister wanted to discuss the real reason for her rejection.

"He's made no offer to me, Lydia," Amelia replied once she gathered herself from the shock of her sister's remark.

"Yes, he did," Lydia continued confidently. "I think you should accept the role of his mistress."

"What? Why would I do that?" Her heart began to pound as Lydia cast her vote in support of the thoughts Amelia had already been considering. The only thing that eased her regret for rejecting Gideon and prevented her from going to him now was the thought of what being his mistress would mean for her sister and Thomas. But if Lydia supported her.... Amelia was scared to give in to the immediate hope kindling in her chest.

"Because you love him. You will always love him. I know you. I know your character. You will spend your life apart from him, loving him, and never be with anyone else. So, be with him. It's not ideal, it's not marriage. But he loves you, too. He wouldn't have shared his deepest held secrets and burdens with you if he didn't. That was real, Amelia. So, be with him."

Lydia was making it sound so easy, so simple. Amelia couldn't believe her sister was encouraging her to do this. To be sure, she voiced the only argument that stopped her these past weeks from doing exactly what Lydia suggested now.

"I would be a mistress, Lydia," Amelia voiced quietly. "This will come back on you and Thomas. Having a whore for a sister."

"Oh, come now," Lydia scoffed. "You could never be a whore. You're devoted to him. And neither Thomas, nor I care about what anyone says or thinks. I just want you to be happy. Thomas wants you to be happy. He thinks it will be through marriage. I know it will only be through the Duke of Birmingham. So, be happy with him. If that's all he can give you now, then very well. Those are his demons, my darling. Not yours. Don't let them or the gossips keep you from your happiness."

The hope blossomed fully in Amelia's chest. She missed him. Desperately. Inconsolably. She felt half herself at all times. All this time without him, watching him and feeling him, but never more. Pretending to give her attention to others, when the cord that bound them together pulled on her ceaselessly.

There was one other issue that dampened her brightening hope. What she had done and said to him the last time they spoke. "He might not accept me," Amelia admitted, remembering. "Not after everything I said to him."

Amelia could see Lydia fight the instinct to insist he would. But after all the broken hopes already weighing on Amelia regarding the Duke of Birmingham, Lydia didn't pile on yet another. Instead of giving her another promise she couldn't trust, Lydia gave her the power of a challenge.

"Try," Lydia said. "You can *try*."

GIDEON

$\mathcal{G}$ ideon nursed his brandy and stared unseeingly at the fire in his study as leaned back in his desk chair. His thoughts were consumed by Amelia. He pretended, each time he saw her, he pretended that he did not know exactly where she was in the room at any given moment. That he did not watch her, did not feel her, did not sense the connection that pulled and strained between them. That he did not care that she may soon be marrying someone else. He pretended and pretended, and the ache had yet to leave him.

But right now, alone and in the dead of night, he let go of the charade and let his sweet, perfect Amelia fill his thoughts openly. Her heart shaped face; the trust and pure faith in him shining in those soft brown eyes; her full lips and their taste; the blush that spread from her face down to her chest; her smiles and teasing and moaning; her unconditional acceptance and support; her steel when he fell short.

He was so lost in the memories of the woman he refused to admit had become his whole world that he did not hear the door open until Lewis spoke. "Miss Amelia Becham, Your Grace."

Gideon stared at him for a moment wondering if he had misheard – if his thoughts were so all-consuming that he had imagined the words that had come out of his butler's mouth. Then the man stepped aside and Amelia entered the room. Lewis left quietly and without comment, shutting the door behind him.

Gideon sprang up from his seat, slamming his glass down on top of his desk in haste. He was around the piece of furniture a moment later, but kept one hand firmly secured to its edge to restrain himself. Because being alone with Amelia for the first time since that fateful day, he wanted nothing more than to go to her, hold her in his arms, beg her forgiveness for breaking his word and her trust, and promise her forever. That vulnerable child within was desperate for him to do exactly that. Right this instant.

He held back, though. Because she was here. At his home. Alone. In the middle of the night. And nothing had changed.

"What's wrong? Are you alright?" His words left him in a rush, his worry forcing them out as fast as possible.

"Yes," her soft, husky voice was music to his ears. He hadn't heard it in weeks. If he heard nothing else for the rest of his days, he would be the happiest man alive. But the dominant part of his mind focused on her, her presence, what she needed. "Yes, I am alright, Your Grace. Nothing is wrong."

"Then what are you doing here?" he asked, the urgency in his voice made clear that he didn't believe her, and why should he? Never before had she come to his home, and after how they had ended things, her presence was all the more peculiar.

"I came to see you," she said honestly. He registered more then. The nervous hope in her eyes. The faint blush to her cheeks. The hesitant pull upwards at the corners of her lips. The hands she clasped in front of her with fingers twitching to fidget.

Gideon felt something in him hardening and taking over.

That part of himself that he hated. The part of him that kept them separated. His hand on the desk curled so tightly into a fist that his knuckles turned white.

"Why?" Now, his voice came out hard.

She swallowed and stepped properly into the room. She seemed prepared for his reaction.

"Thomas and Lydia are getting married in a week," she spoke.

"I am aware. What I am unaware of is why you are here at my home in the middle of the night, alone and completely unchaperoned. Enlighten me." After everything, all he and so many others had done to right her tarnished reputation – as unearned as it may have been– she was here, throwing it all away in a single moment.

"I miss you."

His anger stuttered.

Still. After all this time and all that had passed between them. After he had abandoned her so completely. Still, she was honest. His honest, open Amy.

He shook his head. The fact remained she was here uninvited and unchaperoned, ruining everything. More than just her reputation, but also his efforts at pretending.

"What does that matter?" he ground out. It mattered. It mattered immensely. But he wouldn't tell her that or let her see. He missed her. Wildly. Irrationally. Manically.

She hesitated. His anger making her waver momentarily. But then, she moved closer to him, bridging the gap between them, stopping only a few short feet away. She took a deep breath, visibly gathering herself and her courage, and spoke with conviction.

"It does not," she admitted. "I am here to seek your forgiveness and to be with you. I broke us apart. I let my pride and anger separate us, and I should not have spoken to you so harshly. All the more since I was behaving precisely as you had described. I *was* panting like a whore for you. I would do that and more for you. I had no right to take such offense at you simply naming it.

"The news of the rumor surrounding my family did take me by surprise, but you did not start that, and you are innocent in believing it. How could you not? You did not know me beyond what was said. I do wish you had not been so misinformed, but it does not change how things progressed between us. I may not be a professional, but I am still not a suitable marriage partner for the Duke of Birmingham, regardless of Thomas and Lydia's biased opinions. Your duchess must be well-bred, graceful, and rich in ways that I am not. There are limitations around our relationship outside of our control, which I admit I foolishly forgot as I fell in love with you."

Gideon's chest squeezed, preventing him from drawing in a full breath as he heard those last few words. But she wasn't finished.

"And so, I come here to apologize for how I spoke to you, when your words and intentions were ultimately justified and appropriate, based on false information or not. I do not need to be a wife. I just need to be with *you*. My life would have so much more meaning and joy being with you in any way we can than I could ever have as someone else's wife.

"I am here, alone, unchaperoned, at your home in the middle of the night to ask to be your mistress. I love you and would be honored to be with you. Truly, I do not want to be without you. These weeks apart have been long enough.

"We no longer need worry about finding Lydia a husband, either. As we've established, she and Thomas will be married in a week. I would be so bold, however, as to ask for the other agreements we had made. That you care for me until the end of my days and that I bear our children. I keep a very small household and will ensure I am never a burden on you and the future duchess, should there be one. And you are under no obligation

to continue being with me if you grow tired. But I do not want
to be with anyone else, nor could I rely on Thomas and Lydia or
continue to associate with them. I am willing to contribute to
my household, if that would make you more comfortable. I am
rather gifted at needlework and can provide seamstress
services, but I would ask for your help in disassociating my
reputation from such a business. Other than that, I am yours.
And I wish for you to be mine again."

Speech ended, she paused. The silence was resounding. A
beat passed. Two. Three. Gideon said nothing. He just stood
there, rigid, staring at her. The tension rolled off him in
palpable waves. Amelia hesitated, unsure. It seemed she had not
been prepared for his silence.

Gideon could feel his blood boiling under his skin. He'd
thought he was shocked when she appeared at his door, but
that was nothing compared to what he felt now. And there
was pain. Such a deep, profound ache in his chest, it was hard
to breathe. But he did. He forced air in and out through his
nose as his teeth ground together. He couldn't take his eyes
from her. His exquisite Amelia. The center of his whole
goddamn world. And the rage pounded through him as he
glared at her.

"That was it," she said after another few moments passed in
silence. "That is why I came here. What I came to tell you."

Gideon took a deep breath and exhaled. Forcing the word
through his clenched teeth, he seethed, "Leave."

His heart broke – he admitted as much to himself because
there was no way he could possibly deny the feeling – as he
watched that sweet, open face crumple. He turned away, unable
to bear it, and forced himself to move back behind his desk. He
didn't look at her as he picked up his glass, but he heard the
door close softly. So, so softly.

He drained the entire tumbler in a single gulp, then went to
the side table to refill it, draining that one, too. Refilling it again,

Gideon made himself continue to breathe as the pain and rage ricocheted through his heart and mind.

He'd done it, he thought bitterly. His father would be proud. He'd won. He'd broken her. She had come here to give up her dreams for her life to be with him. He had done exactly what she had accused him of all those weeks ago – he had used her love for him to manipulate her. To seduce her. He forced her into the position he wanted her in. He had vowed to care for her every need, and when he learned the truth of who she really was – or was not – he had abandoned her. Because she didn't fit into what he wanted her to be. He left her and forced *her* to change. He showed her he would be with her in one way and one way only, and if she wanted him, she would make herself fit. He didn't take care of her at all, and now here she was, asking *him* to forgive *her*, forgetting her hopes for her life, her needs, because he had starved her of him. And her need for him, he knew, trumped everything else. Just as his *almost* did for her. Because his need had not outweighed his own stubbornness.

He finished his glass and paced back to the table to fill it again. He hated himself. He had never hated himself more.

And now she'd come here to give him his way. She came to become his mistress. His whore. *His actual whore.* That's what she believed of herself. That's what she believed she was worth to him. And why should she not? He could have married her. He could have fixed everything from the start by marrying her. But he chose not to. He chose to let them both wither while they went about other ways of rectifying her reputation. And because he hadn't married her, here she was, ready to set fire to her perfect reputation anyway. For him. To be with him.

She believed she was not worthy of being his wife. That she deserved only to be his mistress. That he would take another woman as his wife and never be faithful to her. She would cut Thomas and Lydia from her life, knowing the Earl and Countess of Coventry could not keep company with the Duke of Birmingham's whore. Her younger sister would become a *countess*, and she would take up a life where she believed he thought her love a *service* she provided him. That he could tire of and no longer want one day. She would even take up other services if she was too costly to help *him* support her. Because she had to earn her keep with him.

His hand clutched the tumbler so hard that the etching in the crystal cut into his palm, but he barely noticed.

Because he knew, she would be his wife. In everything, she would be a wife to him and consider him her husband, but never say it. She would love him like a wife. Accept him for all his damage and faults. Devote herself completely to him. Be with no other for the rest of her life. She would care for him and ease his burdens. She would do everything in her power to support him. She would bear his children, love them, and raise them. She would be a wife. And would let him call her his mistress.

The glass shattered loudly against the wall. He was disgusted with himself, with everything that he was. He was a coward. A failure. Over and over and over, he failed her. He made promises and said pretty words. But he never made the different choice.

AMELIA

*L*eave.

For five days now, that word and the absolute disgust with which he delivered it had not left Amelia.

She made it out of Gideon's Townhouse that night. Made it back to Coventry House. She didn't tell anyone what transpired. The staff, in all their faithfulness, didn't breathe a word. Lydia and Thomas didn't know, but they noticed her despondency as much as she tried to hide it in the days that followed. They had asked after her. Lydia stayed close. Thomas's attention was tangible.

Amelia hated herself for her failure in hiding her misery. It was unbearably selfish, even if she was trying. They were getting married in two days. Lydia and Thomas should only be thinking of themselves, full of joyous excitement that should be smothering everyone around them. And they were, but they were also clearly worried about her.

Still, she kept at her attempts to hide her heartbreak. She made sure her face was always cheerful, even if she knew they weren't buying it, and pretended she was fine. She had gotten through her failed hopes the first time, she told herself. This was just another turn about the same course. Only at night, when it was just her and her unending loneliness, did she let reality crush her.

Leave. Leave. Leave.

Now, five days later, she sat on the couch in the drawing room alone, putting the final touches on Lydia's gown. The staff were well underway with readying Coventry House for the wedding and packing for their departure directly after. Lydia and Thomas would proceed to their honeymoon, while Amelia would move back to the cottage. She had already written to Walters and Mrs. Nichols to expect her. Amelia had been away from home far too long, and after the whirlwind of the past two months, it was time for her to return to her life.

Lost to the mind-numbing task of finishing Lydia's dress, which she was determined to make perfect, she didn't immediately hear the door opening and others joining her. She looked up to see Lydia following Thomas into the room, a look of dread and anger mingled together on her face. That pulled Amelia fully to the moment, concerned by what put that expression on her sweet, calm sister's face. But she didn't even need to ask.

With horror, she watched as the Duke of Birmingham strode into the room.

She forgot the dress in her lap entirely. She forgot Lydia. She forgot Thomas. All she knew in that moment was the piercing green gaze and harsh beauty focused solely on her without apology. So severe was her shock, she didn't notice how different this was from the past few weeks and how his face was absent of any hostility.

A lifetime passed in a single moment. His gaze swept down her. Not with heat, but with curious concern, as if checking to make sure she was alright. An echo of pain rippled in her chest in response to his scrutiny. His perusal ended where it began, back on her face, and his eyes darkened, brows pinching together. She didn't have time to wonder at it as Thomas spoke, reminding her they weren't alone. Neither one of them pulled their eyes from the other, however.

"We have a guest," he announced unnecessarily. "I forgot to mention, Amelia, I had invited Gideon to spend the next few nights leading up to the wedding with us. He will be my best man during the ceremony."

Amelia felt the blood drain from her face, and she thought she was going to vomit. Her panicked eyes shot to Thomas before turning to Lydia, whose face was thick with displeasure.

Amelia felt lightheaded, getting further and further adrift. Her breaths were coming out rapidly, and she vaguely wondered if she was going to pass out. It was a good thing she was already sitting down, she thought wildly, as she struggled to breathe. She couldn't get a real breath in.

So lost was she in trying to pull in oxygen, she didn't notice Gideon had moved until he was standing directly in front of her. The worry she had glimpsed on his features had deepened dramatically. He took her hand without permission, and the back reaches of her mind registered the current still run through her from the point of contact with his skin. His other hand grasped her elbow, and he urged her to stand, Lydia's dress falling from her lap.

"Look at me," he said.

She couldn't. She couldn't find his face. Couldn't focus on it. Couldn't focus on anything except the struggle to breathe. Her heart was galloping painfully. Like it was determined to break through the confines of her ribs and run for it.

"Amy, *look at me*," his repeated firmly.

It worked. Her eyes found his and stopped. He looked so calm. So in control.

"Breathe," he commanded, his voice and gaze grounding her. She clung to his eyes as he took a deep, exaggerated inhale and she matched it, pulling in her first full breath since the panic set in. She didn't look away. His hand moved from her elbow to brush a lock of hair behind her ear as he instructed, "Again," taking the deep breath with her.

She did his bidding without conscious thought. Finally, her heart started to slow its rhythm.

"That's it, my dear" his low words were soft and soothing as she focused on breathing and calming her heartbeat. "You are alright. Everything is alright. Just breathe."

She felt her eyes fill with cursed tears, and a fresh wave of anger washed away the last of her panic. She blinked rapidly to force the tears away and stepped out of Gideon's hold. She refused to acknowledge the loss she felt from doing so, but her vision clouded again with the evidence. Not fast enough to block out the similar agony flashing across Gideon's features.

She crouched down, picking up the beautiful gown and laying it carefully on the couch before she turned on Thomas.

"What's the meaning of this?" she demanded, her voice breaking with emotion.

"There's no meaning to it," Thomas looked apologetic. "Gideon is my closest friend. I want him to stand with me on my wedding day."

Amelia had no words. She stared at Thomas and wanted to scream. She wanted to scream and rage right in his face. But she couldn't. So, she gathered up the dress, reminding herself to be gentle when her movements came out aggressive. Without a word and with the dress tucked safely in her arms, she rushed to the door.

Gideon didn't speak, nor had he moved. He just watched, but Amelia refused to look at him again.

Leave.

She had to leave. Right this second.

"Where are you going?" Thomas asked, his arrogant ass voice edged with concern that was too late.

She could have hit him.

"Let her go, Thomas," Lydia spoke, her voice quiet with support and understanding.

"But —," Amelia heard Thomas start as she walked into the hall.

"No," Lydia interrupted him firmly. "You made this decision without warning either of us. So, you'll let her go until she's ready."

And then Amelia was out of earshot and didn't know what came next. She went straight to her room, depositing the dress gently on her bed before sitting down next to it.

Leave.

And she fell completely apart.

GIDEON

*G*ideon stared at the doorway Amelia had just run through, listening to the soon-to-be Countess of Coventry dress down Thomas, uncaring of their audience.

God, how he'd hurt her. He'd absolutely crushed that sweet, open, innocent woman he'd spent weeks with. So much so that just the sight of him had thrown her into full-fledged panic. He'd acted on instinct, rushing to her.

Enough was enough. He couldn't do this to her anymore. He was a coward. He'd been a coward for most of his time knowing her. First, unknowingly; then, stubbornly. Because that's what it was. Stubborn pride to believe a happy marriage couldn't exist. Any marriage with Amelia in it *couldn't* be unhappy. And his refusal to marry her, he had finally acknowledged, was his stubborn determination to prove that marriage and love did not coexist in a single relationship. But Genevieve was right. He could let them wither under that forced disbelief, or he could choose something different.

He was ashamed to add to his list of cowardice that he spent the first few days after her midnight visit completely drunk. But then he'd thought of Genevieve's words again, and he finally decided he was done. He was done being a coward. Done hurting her. Done pretending he wasn't uncontrollably and overwhelmingly in love with Amelia Becham.

She knew him. She knew every part of him, even the ones he wished she didn't know. She knew the controlled duke. The broken boy. And these past weeks, she saw his father's cruel son. He wasn't perfect. He wasn't good enough for her. But she saw all of him, accepted each part, and loved him for all that he was.

Gideon was going to be the man she deserved. If he had to work every damned day for the rest of his life to be that man, he would. He was making a different choice. He was choosing to love her unconditionally and unendingly, and he would never let her doubt her worth to him or anyone else ever again. She was the world. His whole world. And he would never let her forget it.

So, he was here. Keeping his promise to Thomas to stay at Coventry House for the wedding and to make things right with Amelia. Judging by the past ten minutes since he arrived, however, it would be significantly harder than he'd anticipated. That was understandable and acceptable. He would do everything and anything she needed for as long as it would take. She was all that mattered.

Lydia finally addressed him, pulling him out of his reverie. "Should I go to her, Your Grace?" her tone was polite, but he could hear the distrust, disapproval, and curiosity layered heavily within it. She had eyed him with similar feelings when he'd initially been shown to the library where she and Thomas were reading and working.

Her question, however, took him by surprise. Even though she didn't trust him and was clearly upset with him – and it wasn't difficult to figure out why – she was deferring to him on how to proceed with Amelia. Hopefully, that meant her disapproval didn't run so deep that she would oppose their match or try to talk Amelia out of trusting him again.

"No," he pulled his eyes to the scowling bride. "She'll seek us out when she's ready." He was confident in his answer. The comfort of others, even her sister, would be unwelcome to Amelia right now. The way she panicked, the way she ran out, not making eye contact with anyone – her needs had been clear. She needed to be alone. She would come out when she no longer needed that.

And she did. Not an hour later, she reentered the drawing room. Thomas sat on the couch, Gideon next to him in the armchair watching the door, as they drank their tea, neither one of them attempting conversation. Gideon's mind had been upstairs with Amelia, and Thomas was focused on his bride, who was pointedly ignoring him as she played at the piano.

Gideon was the first out of his seat when Amelia walked in, shooting up as if he'd been sitting on an open flame. Thomas was slower to stand, and Lydia quietly called her sister's name before going to her and grasping her hands.

"Darling, are you alright?" Lydia's voice was concerned.

Amelia was careful not to look in Gideon's direction, but he could see the puffiness of her eyes and the redness surrounding them. He hated that he'd made her cry yet again. "Yes, I'm fine," she said unconvincingly. "I apologize for my outburst. You are most welcome, Your Grace." She angled her head towards him when she said the last part, but still kept her eyes averted.

"Amelia, I'm sorry," Thomas started.

"It's fine, Thomas," the snap of her voice was in direct contrast to its civil politeness immediately before.

"It's not," he insisted, and Amelia looked at him.

She read something in his face before sighing and saying, "You are not wrong for wanting someone important to you to stand with you at your wedding."

"I should have told you, though."

"Yes," both Lydia and Amelia replied.

"Yes, you should have," Amelia continued. "But it's done now, and everything is fine."

Thomas's face twisted, the regret clear on his features. He strode to Amelia and wrapped her in his arms. A beat passed before she hugged him back.

"I am truly sorry, sister," Gideon heard him murmur, and his chest clenched, again berating himself for the past and how enormously he'd mistaken their very obvious relationship.

"It's okay, Thomas," came Amelia's soft reply in that husky voice he loved.

Gideon cleared his throat. "Would you care for some tea, Miss Becham?" he asked.

"No, thank you, Your Grace," she answered, her voice solid. She stepped out of Thomas's embrace, but still stood facing him and Lydia. "I would like some air. Lydia, would you care to join me in the garden?"

"Of course," Lydia replied without hesitation, stepping forward and linking arms with her sister.

"May we all join you?" Thomas asked.

"Yes," Amy replied before steering Lydia towards the outside door.

"Well, I'm good and in the doghouse, I'd say," Thomas muttered to Gideon as they followed the ladies.

"I'd say so," Gideon agreed, stepping outside. "Why didn't you tell them I was coming to stay?"

"I knew they'd both be displeased."

"I guess we're both cowards, then," Gideon commented.

Thomas looked at him with interest as they moved through the greenery of the Coventry House garden. "Oh?" he said. "And how are you a coward, Birmingham?"

Gideon gave his friend a wry look. "You know how," he answered.

"I see," was all Thomas said, but Gideon could see the earl's mind working.

They were quiet for a moment as they trailed the women, and then Thomas spoke again. "Would you like to walk with Amelia?" he asked directly.

Gideon gave his friend an assessing look, surprised he would trust him with Amelia again. He answered plainly, "Yes."

"Wait here," Thomas instructed and then hurried forward to talk to the ladies. Gideon saw Amelia's back stiffen and both Thomas and Lydia look to her. After an agonizing moment, she nodded, and Thomas turned back to him, nodding, as well – but Gideon was already striding forward.

AMELIA

*A*melia heard the Duke of Birmingham approaching. Thomas and Lydia had already moved on, talking privately. She waited, tense, for Gideon to reach her. When he did, he offered her his arm. She took it, ignoring the shiver of awareness that came from touching him. They were silent as they fell into step.

She focused on breathing and keeping her eyes forward. One step in front of the other. These little things were all that mattered. Not the man beside her whose arm she held. Not the smell of spice and warmth burrowing into her chest. Not the loss, loneliness, pain. Just her breathing and walking forward.

"I miss you, too," the deep velvet voice was low and reverberating, and she felt it trail across the back of her neck, making the hairs stand on end.

Her fingers tightened on his forearm reflexively, her heart rate picking up.

"When you came to me the other night," he continued, not waiting for her to respond. His words were stilted with an agony she'd never heard in them before. That had her angling her head just slightly towards him. He cleared his throat and

continued. "I didn't know what to do. I had already been struggling, day in and day out, minute by minute, staying away from
you. Watching you. And pretending everything was normal.
That I wasn't holding myself together through sheer stubbornness and arrogant pride."

He paused to lead them to a bench they'd come upon in the
small garden, unwrapping her arm from around his but keeping
hold of her hand as they sat.

"And then you came to me," he continued, his emerald eyes
burning into her with his earnestness. "I swear to you, Amelia, I
had never felt such worry in my life as I did in that moment
when you walked through the door. My mind cycled through so
many different awful scenarios that could have brought you to
me, risking such scandal.

"But then you said what you said. You told me why you were
there. What you had chosen for your life for the sake of me and
my stubborn, cowardly pride." The venom in his voice was
heavy. Amelia turned to him fully, watching his face as he spoke,
but it was his turn not to meet her gaze. He stared off into the
garden as he continued.

"I had been hating myself more than you could ever imagine
after how I treated you, what I tried to force you into, and then
how I abandoned you and kept us apart when you demanded
my respect. For you to then come to me and take that burden
onto yourself, to make yourself smaller – tossing aside your
hopes, dreams, name, family, reputation, *everything* – when I
vowed to care for you…." His voice trailed off as he swallowed
audibly.

"I needed you to leave," he said, his deep voice quiet and so,
so pained. "Because I have never loathed myself more than I did
in that moment and every moment since. And that loathing has
no place in the same room as you."

He looked at her, then. What she saw in his eyes made her
breath catch. "You are everything, Amy. The center of my world.

The only thing that means anything. And I have failed you in so many ways. At every corner. I do not deserve you or your forgiveness for all I've done, the pain I've caused you, the ways that I have failed you. But I seek it anyway. Because I love you. More dearly and madly than I could have ever imagined or hoped for. You are the most precious thing there has ever been, and I cannot live without you."

Amelia didn't second guess it. His love and sincerity settling into her as an absolute, and she was unwavering in her decision of what came next. Without a word, she placed a hand on his cheek. His skin was rough and warm under hers. He didn't say anything, just kept his crystal eyes pinned to hers. She leaned forward and kissed him. She didn't care who was there to witness it. If Thomas and Lydia still strolled around the garden or the staff watched. All she cared about was kissing the man she loved and was sure she'd lost. The man who loved her.

Her heart was full, and she wanted to weep for joy at what he confessed to her. He loved her, and there was nothing else in the world that mattered save that.

His hand came up to cover hers as he kissed her back, letting her guide it, until she pulled away, barely an inch from his lips. She met his emerald eyes again and whispered, her breath mingling with his, "You will come to me tonight?"

His gaze was reverent as he nodded, confident and sure. She smiled then on a small laugh, no longer able to suppress the tears of happiness, and this time, he kissed her. His hand came to her waist and pulled her as close as he could in their seated position, while hers moved into his hair. He kissed her with so much emotion, it seemed he couldn't take anymore when he finally broke the kiss and buried his head in her neck, hugging her close instead.

Amelia had never been happier. She wrapped her arms around him, smiling unabashedly as she eagerly envisioned the rest of their life. Starting tonight.

GIDEON

*G*ideon walked quietly down the hall towards the room Amelia had pointedly entered earlier. He couldn't believe how he deserved her and how she had forgiven him without a thought after everything. He would not let down the faith she put in him again. He would treasure and protect it with everything he had. Just as he would love her and never intentionally make her cry anything but tears of joy ever again. It had made his heart soar when she laughed with those tears in her eyes, and that smile on her face. She glowed with joy. Like she couldn't believe it. And neither could he.

He couldn't believe that the loveliest woman he'd ever known was meant for him on such an intrinsic level. That she fit him and fulfilled him so perfectly. And after the turmoil of the past weeks and their confusion, misunderstandings, pain, she was still his. She would always be his. And she accepted him. He was hers.

The night couldn't come fast enough. When Amelia invited Gideon to her tonight, he knew she needed him. The truth was, he needed her, too. To hold her, love her, reassure himself that they were no longer apart.

Coming up to the door, Gideon tapped his hand on the wood quietly. Not a full breath later, the door opened, and he hurried in. She must have been waiting just inside for how quickly it opened.

He closed to the door behind him, careful not to make a noise. Then, he turned around and all thoughts left his head.

Amelia was a vision. She stood there, looking simultaneously confident and shy, her burnt golden mane down in waves around her face. She was dressed in only her nightgown with her dressing gown open in front. Gideon had never seen a more beautiful sight than Amelia in this moment. Open, trusting, offering him herself.

As if to further that point, before Gideon could say or do anything, Amelia let her dressing gown fall to the floor. Then, face flushed and looking radiant, chocolate eyes never leaving his, she pulled her nightgown over each shoulder and shrugged it down, until it, too, pooled at her feet.

Gideon's mouth went dry. His eyes raked over those luscious, naked curves that his hands craved to touch, before moving back to her face. She watched him with unfaltering love and trust. The trust it had killed him to lose these past weeks and that now saved him with its return.

He didn't miss the shyness peeking through Amelia's eyes either. In the space of two heartbeats, he had his hand on the back of her neck and his lips on hers. His other hand grasped the delicious curves at her waist and pulled her body flush against him and his already hard length.

He'd never kissed her like this. Even that awful day when he learned the magnitude of his mistakes, he'd kissed her seductively, possessively. Tonight, he kissed her savagely. Greedily. Without a shadow of restraint. As if kissing her, touching her, feeling her – it was all there was in life. She was a feast, and he was starved.

Both of her hands were in his hair, and she tugged at the

strands gently. His chest rumbled from the pleasure of it. She arched her body into him and kissed him back just as desperately. Like she needed him just as much as he needed her. Like he was her sustenance, too.

His hand at the back of her neck squeezed before moving into her hair. Just like every other time, the action triggered her body to melt in his hands, and he used his grasp on her roots to angle her head just right and deepen the kiss.

The moan she rewarded him with shot straight through his cock, and he ground against her instinctively. She tore her mouth from his, gasping. He didn't stop, immediately moving his mouth down the column of her neck, while the hand at her waist moved to her breast and began teasing it.

"Your…." Her voice was a breath of air. "Your Grace…," she started.

Gideon snapped his head up, his grip on her hair tightening to inflict just the right hint of pain. He got the desired result – she opened her eyes and looked at him. Her glazed look of lust made him strain still further in the confines of his clothing.

"*Gideon*," his voice was a command.

She shuddered, her eyes rolling back in her head. That reaction pleased him immensely. He loosened his grip on her but still kept a firm hold.

"Gideon," she corrected, her voice huskier with her arousal.

He continued cupping her breast while watching her. He pinched her nipple, rolling it between his fingers, and she arched into him. She was lost completely to him, and he was still fully clothed and had barely touched her.

"Yes, dear?" he pitched his voice low, letting it rumble out of him.

"I need…." She broke off in a moan.

"Yes, Amy? What do you need?"

"I…I don't know. More. Please, Gideon."

That cracked through his own crazed desire enough for him

to remember. He was moments away from fucking her against the nearest flat surface. That was not how he wanted this first time to go.

Gideon leaned in to kiss her again, slower this time but just as thorough. He bent down, lifting her off the ground with one arm under her knees, the other supporting her back. Her arms encircled his shoulders. Gideon didn't resist biting that lusciously full bottom lip as he carried her to the bed and murmured, "I'll take care of you, my dear."

AMELIA

*A*melia wasn't a person anymore. She was pure sensation.

Everything about her zeroed in on Gideon's hands on her, her blood coursing through her, the heat pooling within her, the ache…. Oh, that deep, deep ache that she couldn't identify but needed satisfied. She knew Gideon would ease it. She needed him. More of him. More of everything that was happening. More, more, more.

He deposited her gently on the bed, and she pulled herself back to its center, not taking her eyes off him. He didn't join her on the bed. Instead, he looked at her with such intense heat in his eyes, she had to bite back another moan. He wasn't even touching her. He was just looking at her, and she was at his mercy.

He started undressing, and with each item of clothing he removed, he watched her reaction. Her mouth watered. She couldn't imagine a more perfect man. She catalogued the muscles he revealed one by one. His tan skin with light dustings of hair. She drank in the sight of him, and when he finally revealed what she had felt against her on multiple occasions now, she instinctively licked her lips.

My God, he was beautiful. Every inch of him. The most beautiful sight she'd ever seen. She itched to run her fingers and then her mouth over those hard ridges and muscles. Memorize the feel of them. She wanted to grasp the hard length of him and please him as he guided her. She wanted to explore that magnificent body and sear it into her mind so she knew it as well as her own.

He climbed over to her, and she laid back as he covered her body with his own.

"You're so beautiful," she told him reverently, her fingers coming up to gently trace along the muscles of his chest.

He met her eyes before kissing her again. Her hands had a mind of their own as they continued to run across his chest, his shoulders, his back. His skin was hot to touch, his muscles firm under her fingers.

He moved out of her grasp, lowering himself down her body. He kissed her sensitive breasts, licking and biting until she quivered beneath him. Her hands fell to the sheets, and she fisted them in her grip, surrendering to the feel of him.

"So perfect," he murmured, his deep voice hoarse from his desire. She could feel his warm breath on her stomach as he continued moving further down.

"Your…." She stopped, correcting herself again. "Gideon. What are you doing?"

"Shh," he kissed her stomach. "Do you know I love you, Amy?"

"Yes," it came out as a moan. Just the thought of this strong, resilient, confident man loving her, being soft and warm for her, caring for her…. It pushed her further along the wave her body was steadily climbing.

He rubbed his lips over the skin below her belly button. "Do you trust me?"

"Implicitly," she answered without hesitation.

She could feel his smile against her skin, and then he moved with purpose. A moment later, he was pushing her legs apart and nestling his shoulders between them.

Her heart pounded in her chest, but she didn't ask what he was doing again. She leaned into his love and her trust, just like he'd intended her to with his questions.

And then his mouth was on her, and she was gone. His tongue ran up her entrance in a long, steady stroke before he wrapped his lips around her clit. He started off light and teasing. Her body arched off the bed, and he wrapped one hand behind her back to keep her lifted up and angled to him. The other stayed planted on her thigh, holding her open. His tongue flicked and teased before becoming more insistent. He bit down gently and pushed her further, further, further.

She writhed against him as the pressure built, powerful, unstoppable. The ache for him was all-consuming, and still his mouth did not cease. It wasn't until her body started trembling violently that he finally removed his hand from her back and pushed a single finger into her, stroking. Pleasure rocketed through her. The sounds coming out of her were unholy, and she didn't care.

It was close. So close, so close, so close. But not enough.

"Gideon," she panted. "*Gideon….*" It was all she could say. The only thought left in her mind apart from the agonizing pleasure coursing through her.

He added a second finger, stretching her further, before he curled them both inside her. A heavy moan pulled from deep within her chest. Her muscles were coiled so tight, she was sure she was going to rip apart.

Gideon pulled his mouth from her only for a moment.

"Let go, Amy," he instructed gently in his soft gravel voice, and it pushed her completely over the edge she had been climbing since he first kissed her. She exploded. Her blood pounded through her, reaching the edges of her fingertips, her toes, her lips.

Her body collapsed back to the bed, and he gently kissed the inside of her thigh before crawling back up to align himself with her entrance. She looked at him through hooded eyes and found the crystal green of his on absolute fire for her.

"So stunning," he whispered before his firm lips were on her again, and the taste of her mixed with him filled her with wanton pleasure. She grabbed at him, unable to get close enough. She wanted to devour him, pull him right into herself.

He growled, ratcheting her wild desire to a fever pitch.

Everything she'd felt so far was amazing, but it still wasn't enough. If anything, she was more ravenous than before. She needed more. She needed him. She needed *closer*.

She felt his cock nudging at her center, and she pulled away from his kiss to moan, "*Yes*."

Her word unleashed him. Gideon pushed forward and finally, *finally*, sank into her. That gorgeous, mouthwatering cock stretched her so deliciously, she almost lost her mind. He must have thought so, too, because he groaned so deeply and uncontrollably, she nearly climaxed from the sound alone. She knew she would become addicted to hearing the sounds of his pleasure.

He was still being gentle, she realized somewhere in the back of her mind, his movements slow and shallow. He wasn't even fully inside her yet. She understood why a moment later when his strokes came up against resistance. She stiffened at the pinching sensation, but he was there immediately. Kissing her deeply, devastatingly. His hand kneading her breast. His fingers rolling her nipple. His teeth biting her lip. His body covering hers. His scent overwhelming her. She turned to liquid under the onslaught, completely lost to him.

Sensing the moment she relaxed, Gideon shifted his hips and pushed through the barrier within her, causing the pinch to turn sharp, and seated himself fully. She pulled her mouth from his and gasped, scrunching her face.

But Gideon became ruthless. Once he had broken through, he set a punishing rhythm. Circling his hips, he pushed her quickly through the pain until she felt nothing but pleasure and the fullness of him inside her.

She ran her lips along his collarbone, kissing and licking. He hooked one her legs over his arm, pulling it up, and the new angle had him hitting a spot within her that turned her moans into screams. He covered her mouth with his and swallowed the sounds, not stopping or slowing his pace. She began to match his rhythm, her hips meeting his. One of her hands dug into the muscles of his arms, while the other reached up and grabbed the pillow in an iron grip.

"Fuck, you're so tight," he growled as he continued to slam into her.

She began shaking again as he drove her closer and closer to the edge with each of his deep thrusts.

Gideon buried his head in her neck with a groan that tickled the sensitive skin behind her ear. "Again, Amy. Come for me again." His voice was aggressively rough, and it was the most erotic sound she'd ever heard. She came undone with a cry of his name, her body clenching down hard on his as he moved inside her.

He made a sound deep in his chest as her climax set off his. He sank his teeth into the skin at the base of her neck as his cock twitched and he pumped his release inside her.

Quiet.

Gideon's head stayed buried in the crook of her neck as they floated down. He kissed over his bite, releasing her leg, and then raised himself up to look into her eyes. They were both sweaty and panting, and he gently brushed the hair back from her face before cupping her cheek.

He was looking at her with such tenderness, Amelia's chest

hurt from how full her heart felt. As if the organ could no longer fit inside her own body. Turning her head, she kissed the palm of his hand. She looked deep into the emerald green eyes of the most handsome, kind, strong, damaged man she'd ever met. The eyes that pulled her in and bound her to him the very moment they had met hers. She could live and die in his gaze. She hoped she would.

"I love you, Gideon Edwards."

GIDEON

*G*ideon lay staring at the ceiling with Amelia's head resting on his chest and his hand tracing circles along her spine. Her warm vanilla scent soothed him. He couldn't remember ever feeling so content. So at peace and in love. And this amazing, wonderful, stunning woman wanted his love. Took it all in and gave him hers in return.

Of course, he'd known for a long time that she loved him, even before she'd first said it. She'd been showering him with her love for almost as long as he'd known her. She hadn't said it until that night she came to him at his Townhouse, and it had made his breath leave him when she did. But hearing it tonight.... For no other reason than just to say, just to love him in their happiness together. The warmth that spread through him at the sound of those five words in that low, husky voice, it was indescribable. He'd never experienced anything like it.

"I will talk to Thomas tomorrow," he said into the quiet night.

"About what?" she asked sleepily. He smiled at the sound, unable to rein in the fiercely male pride he felt at wearing her out so thoroughly. He couldn't wait to wear her out in every possible way he could imagine.

"To ask for his permission," he replied.

Her head snapped up. No longer lethargic, she looked at him with her brow furrowed deeply in confusion.

"What?" she asked.

"What?" he repeated.

"His permission for what, Gideon?" Amelia pushed to sit up fully, not bothering to cover herself.

"For your hand, of course," he answered, sitting up, too. "I was planning to wait until after the wedding, so as not to distract from their day. And truthfully, I imagined I'd need more time to beg your forgiveness. Down on hand and knee if need be – it's no less than I deserve. But after tonight, I don't think it wise to wait."

"Gideon," she shook her head, her distress clearly growing.

Gideon watched her struggle. He rubbed her back comfortingly, and his voice was warm, gentle, and sure when he asked, "What's the matter, my dear?"

"But I am your mistress," she looked at him with confusion and what looked oddly like fear on her face. As if he was rejecting her – which made absolutely no sense.

"You are not my mistress, Amy," he said firmly. "You will be my wife. I will never have a mistress or be with anyone else but you for the rest of my life."

She looked down, shaking her head, and pulled the sheet up to cover herself.

He couldn't understand it. Unless…. Unless she didn't believe him? Unless she thought he would change his mind on his way to marrying her and then she wouldn't be his anything. Was that it?

He lifted her chin, forcing her to meet his eyes with her soft brown ones. "What is the matter?" he repeated, adding more of his dominance to the soft command.

"I am content, Gideon," she told him quietly, truthfully. "I don't want to lose what we have, lose *you*, trying to gain something more. I just want to be with you. I don't care about marriage."

This was it. The difficulty wasn't in obtaining her forgiveness. No, it was in this. In showing her what she meant to him, what she was worth. Gideon felt the now familiar ache of regret in his chest. She still didn't believe herself worthy of being his wife. So much so that she thought she would lose him again at the prospect of it. That she *could* lose him at all.

There was nothing for it. He couldn't undo the past, but he could be the man she deserved going forward and give her the solid footing she needed to never doubt her feet again.

"What did I tell you all those weeks ago, Amy?" His voice was hard but not without warmth. "What am I to you?"

She hesitated before answering. "You are mine."

"And what are you to me?"

"I am yours."

"And what will I always do?"

"Take care of me, my needs, without apology or reservation." He couldn't hold back the pleased smile that pulled at his lips.

"And what will you always do?"

She hesitated another moment, but then said, "Trust in us."

"I broke my word before and failed you. I have made you doubt your worth to me and the permanency of my love," he cupped her face. "But let me be clear now. You are the most beautiful, most exquisite thing in my world, and always will be. There is no one richer, brighter, more perfect for me, nor will there ever be. There is no better wife for me; mistress for my bed; mother for my children; duchess for my house; sister for my sister; love for my life. I don't know how you were made for me, or I for you, but you were, and you have gathered the pieces of my broken and scarred soul and rebuilt it whole and healed.

"I had been so sure there was no happiness to be found in

marriage after seeing nothing but pain, loss, hatred, and indifference in my parents' marriage. In their treatment of Genevieve and me. But you, my sweet Amelia, have shown me that won't be true of my marriage. That a man can love his wife like she is the center of all things. The most precious, most important thing of his life. His strength, his heart, his soul. Because you are, Amy. All that and more.

"I will never fail you or make you doubt yourself again. I will never abandon you. I will never put my needs or my stubbornness before you and your needs, because caring for you and loving you *is* my greatest need. So, I guess, yes, you will be my mistress. My whore in our bedroom. And I will be yours. I will love you, care for you, cherish you, and want none but you for all our days and after. There is no one that could ever be anything more for me than you. You, my soon-to-be wife, are my everything."

Her lip trembled as she stared unblinkingly into his eyes. He let her see his sincerity, determination, and love – all of it, uncensored and unfaltering. She lost her composure completely as a sob escaped her. Covering her face with her hands, she let the sheet fall to her lap and cried. Gideon did not hesitate. Pulling her to him, he wrapped his arms around her and kissed the top of her head, while her cries mixed oddly with laughter.

She lifted her face back up, not bothering to wipe her tears.

"You want to marry me?" she repeated, another laugh joyously escaping with her words.

"More than anything." Amusement played in his eyes even as his face and voice remained serious. "I must confess, I did already tell Genevieve without first asking you, but we can remedy that right now. Won't you be my duchess, my dear?"

She laughed outright, her happiness overflowing, and kissed him then, the salt of her tears making it all the sweeter.

EPILOGUE

9 months later

"You three really need to stop this," Gideon grumbled, annoyed, as he helped Amelia up the steps of the Coventry Estate.

"I like it," Genevieve commented from behind them. "And Adelaide is so sweet. I love seeing her."

"You're not helping, Genevieve," Gideon muttered, displeased.

"What's there to help with?" Amelia asked, letting Gideon guide her unnecessarily to the entrance. He had been adamant about helping her with everything. She was certain it would become a bit trying very soon, but she also cherished his over-solicitousness. And she might have already coordinated with Genevieve to help keep him in check when it became too much.

Genevieve was still such a quiet and observant girl, but with Amelia's love, Thomas and Lydia's friendship, and the growth of their family, she had been blossoming. She had opened up more to show how wise, fierce, and loving she truly was and how much her dry humor matched that of her brother's. The change in her over the past several months filled both Amelia and Gideon with pride.

"Stopping these nonsense visits," Gideon seethed through clenched teeth as they entered the Estate. He clearly did not appreciate the women not taking him seriously. "You're about ready to burst and still we have to take a difficult carriage ride over here for a meal."

"She's fine, brother," Genevieve removed her cloak. "Good day, Hughes."

"Your Graces," Hughes greeted them, shutting the door. "Miss Edwards," he smiled affectionately at her.

Gideon nodded at him, and Amelia smiled her greeting.

"Accept it, Gideon," Amelia said to her husband as he helped her with her cloak. Hughes began leading Genevieve towards where Thomas, Lydia, and their newborn daughter waited for them. "You have a large, loving family now. And it will be good for the children, too," she rubbed her swollen belly. "They can all grow up together and keep the tradition going when they are the adults."

Before Amelia could take a step away from him, Gideon's hands grabbed her wrists from behind. His grip was firm and at the edge of painful, eliciting the effect he desired. She let out a small whimper and leaned back into him, completely pliant.

He smirked, bending down to nuzzle her neck and trace over her rapid pulse with his lips. She angled her head, giving him better access. He kissed her, biting down lightly, and she pushed her backside against his stiffening cock.

"I guess I will have to accept it," he pitched his voice into the low, seductive timbre that he knew intensified her arousal. Her breath began coming out in quiet pants. Gideon smiled like the devil himself, loving how responsive she was to him. He bit her earlobe, and she moaned. "And I guess you'll have to accept being wet for me for the next few hours without any release, won't you?" He kissed that tender spot behind her ear before letting go of her wrists and stepping around to stand beside her.

Amelia's eyes were hooded, giving Gideon a deep sense of satisfaction. He rubbed a hand warmly where his child was growing before offering her his arm. Amelia could only blink at him with soft, glazed eyes. She looked at him like he was still the beginning, middle, and end of her whole world. Gideon couldn't help it. He leaned forward and planted a soft kiss to her full, pouted lips before taking her hand and tucking it into the crook of his elbow.

Leading them forward, he noted the empty entryway and the door Hughes had left ajar for them before discreetly giving the Duke and Duchess of Birmingham their privacy.

"That was mean, Gideon," that husky feminine voice whispered as Amelia came out of the fog of arousal Gideon had created.

"Don't worry, my dear wife," Gideon laughed quietly. "When I get you home, I'll fuck you like my mistress needs to be fucked."

Soft brown eyes met emerald green ones in a powerful mix of mischief, passion, and unimaginable love.

"Do you promise?"

The End

ACKNOWLEDGMENTS

This story has been a few years in the making. Thank you to Addie for inspiring me to bring this out of the "to be written" pile and believing it could make it into the hands of readers.

Thank you to Ayushi and Maddi for their feedback and honest opinions on this piece.

To Kristin, thank you for encouragement and the awesome photos in preparation for this book.

A very special thank you to Luisa for her patience, creative feedback, and collaboration in capturing my vision with such a beautiful cover design.

Thank you to the teams at Torch Lit Ink and Booked with the Emilys for your help in getting my book out there to my readers.

To Sierra and David at the Bookery, thank you for believing in me and your support.

My booksta girlies and guys! I see you. Thank you for seeing me.

And to my husband. Thank you for always being my number one fan. I love you.

ABOUT THE AUTHOR

K.P. March is a lover of literature, books, and the art of writing. She loves to lose herself in writing and reading books of dark romance, historical romance, romantasy, and fantasy, and she is an absolute sucker for happy endings. She studied Elizabethan Lit and holds a Ph.D. in Writing Studies. *The Mistress* is her debut novel and the first installment of the *Foxgloves Regency Romance Series*. Originally from New Jersey, she now lives in the Cincinnati-area with her husband and three cats.

Follow K.P. March at:
www.authorkpmarch.com
www.instagram.com/authorkpmarch